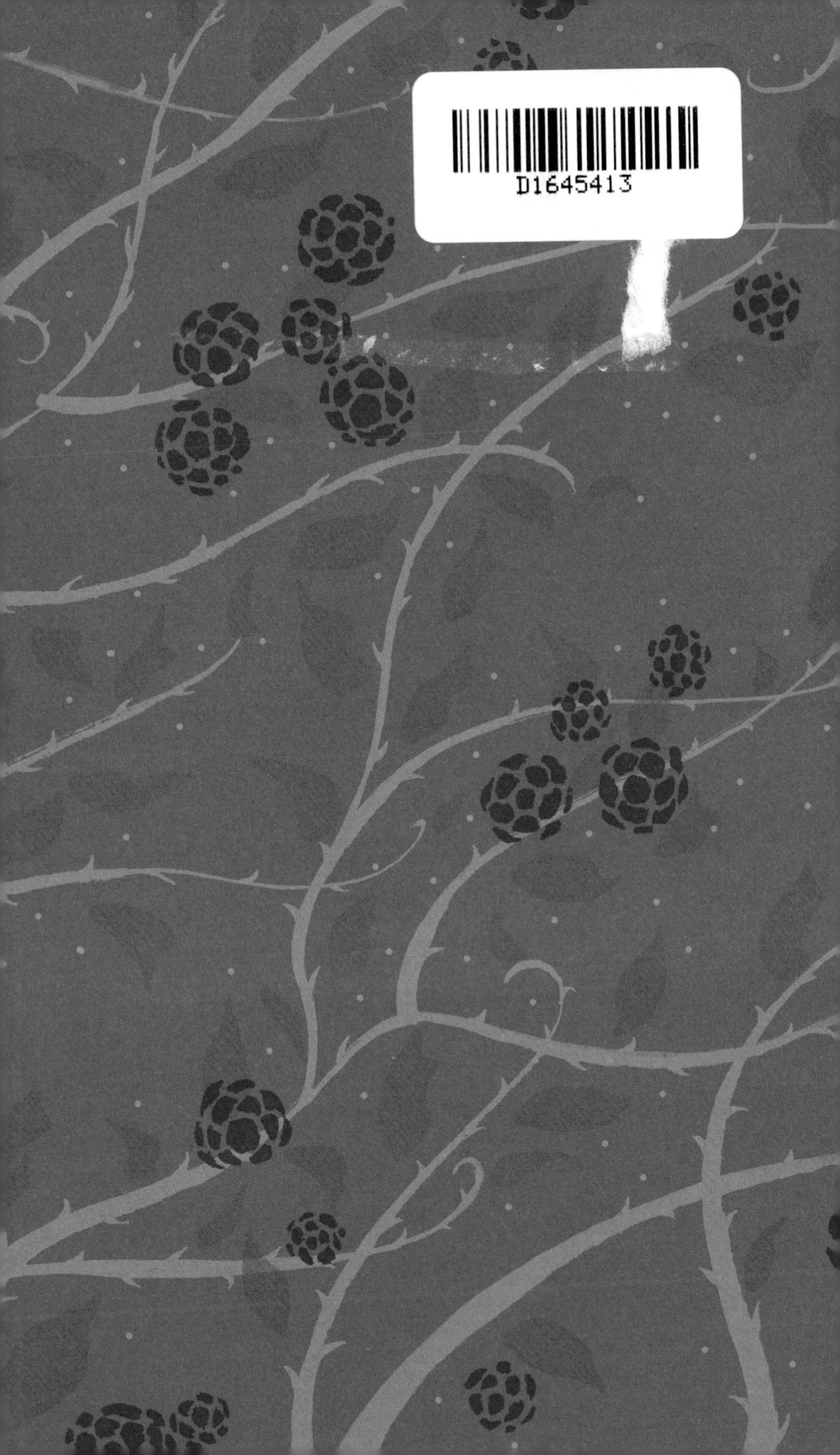

'A superb feat of storytelling.'
Hilary McKay, author of *The Skylarks' War*

'Thrilling historical action . . .
One of her finest novels to date.'
Bookseller

'Carroll's most compelling book yet.'
Ross Montgomery, author of *The Midnight Guardians*

'With the power of her pen, Emma Carroll
makes history come alive.'
Scott Evans, *The Reader Teacher* & #PrimarySchoolBookClub

'An intriguing plot, endearing characters and originality
by the bucket load. Wonderful!'
Lesley Parr, author of *The Valley of Lost Secrets*

'An absolute triumph!'
Book Lover Jo

'Superb. A very moving book.'
Perdita Cargill

'Carroll is a brilliant author.'
Independent Book Reviews

'I never know what Emma Carroll's going to write next
but I always know I'm going to love it.'
Jenny McLachlan, author of *The Land of Roar*

'An utter triumph.'
Judith Eagle, author of *The Pear Affair*

FABER has published children's books since 1929. T. S. Eliot's *Old Possum's Book of Practical Cats* and Ted Hughes' *The Iron Man* were amongst the first. Our catalogue at the time said that 'it is by reading such books that children learn the difference between the shoddy and the genuine'. We still believe in the power of reading to transform children's lives. All our books are chosen with the express intention of growing a love of reading, a thirst for knowledge and to cultivate empathy. We pride ourselves on responsible editing. Last but not least, we believe in kind and inclusive books in which all children feel represented and important.

About the Author

Once told by poet Ted Hughes her writing was 'dangerous', it took Emma Carroll twenty years of English teaching and a life-changing cancer diagnosis to feel brave enough to give her dream of being an author a try. Nowadays, she's a bestselling author and the 'Queen of Historical Fiction' (*BookTrust*). She has been nominated for and the winner of numerous national, regional and schools awards – including the Books Are My Bag Readers' Award, Branford Boase, CILIP Carnegie Medal, Young Quills, Teach Primary and the Waterstones Book Prize. Emma's home is in the Somerset hills with her husband and two terriers. She still can't believe her luck that she gets to write dangerous books for a living.

By the Same Author

Frost Hollow Hall
The Girl Who Walked on Air
In Darkling Wood
The Snow Sister
Strange Star
Letters from the Lighthouse
Secrets of a Sun King
When We Were Warriors
The Somerset Tsunami

The Week at World's End

EMMA CARROLL

faber

First published in 2021
by Faber & Faber Limited
Bloomsbury House,
74–77 Great Russell Street,
London WC1B 3DA
faberchildrens.co.uk

Typeset in Garamond Premier by MRules
Printed by CPI Group (UK) Ltd, Croydon CR0 4YY

A CIP record for this book
is available from the British Library

ISBN 978–0–571–36443–5

2 4 6 8 10 9 7 5 3 1

Mankind must put an end to war or war will put an end to mankind.

JOHN F. KENNEDY, PRESIDENT OF THE UNITED STATES OF AMERICA 1961–1963

Bombs do not choose – they hit everything.

NIKITA KHRUSHCHEV, PREMIER OF THE SOVIET UNION 1958–1964

Day One

US PRESIDENT WARNS CUBA: MISSILES COULD LEAD TO WAR

The Daily Times, Tuesday 23 October 1962

1

It was after tea on a school night when I found the dead body. I'd gone out to the shed to fill up the coal bucket, which was as good an excuse as any to escape our kitchen for a moment's peace. Being a Tuesday, we'd had just pie and mash for tea, and being a day with a 'y' in it, my big sister Bev was arguing about why it wasn't her turn to do the dishes. Our terrier Flea, an excellent listener, was waiting patiently for any leftover pie. And all Mum did was turn the radio up louder. It was that new Beatles song again, the one that went '*Love, love me do*', which, with the clatter of plates and smell of mashed potato, was giving me a headache.

Outside, the evening was inky black. The air had a bite of frost to it, and the only sounds were the distant hum of cars, and next door's water gurgling down the drain. I stood for a moment, enjoying how peaceful it was to not hear Bev yakking on, or the radio playing hit song after hit song because Mum, who hated silence, had barely switched it off since Dad died.

I went down the two steps to the shed and opened the door, only now switching on my torch. I was checking for spiders, mostly, and certainly wasn't expecting anything else to appear in the torchlight. But it did. Something woolly and green. A bobble hat.

I took a tiny step closer. My heart began to thunder.

The hat was on a person's head.

They were lying against the coal heap, facing the far wall. All I could see was the jut of a cheekbone. A coat collar turned up against the cold. A muddy hand that looked more like a freshly dug potato than anything human. The person wasn't moving: they were either very fast asleep . . .

Or dead.

I backed out of the shed faster than any spider could make me move. With the door shut and bolted, I caught my breath. I tried to think. The sensible thing would be to go straight back inside and tell Mum, who'd rush round to our next-door neighbours and ask to use their telephone to call the police.

But I'd never seen a dead body. And I was curious for a look – just quickly, just to be sure – though I was far too scared to go back in the shed by myself. So I did the unsensible thing: I went across the street to my best friend Ray's. He'd never seen a dead body, either, and I knew he'd be up for it, given half a chance.

*

It took Ray ages to come to the door. I'd started shivering by now – the shock, I supposed, and excitement and the cold, because I'd come out without a coat. My finger hovered over the doorbell. Obviously Ray was in, because the television was on and I could hear his sister's annoying laugh through the glass. I was about to press the bell again, when he opened the door.

'At last!' I cried.

'What's up?' Ray looked a bit put out, as if I was interrupting something.

'You need to come over to mine,' I told him. 'Like, *now*!'

I couldn't say any more when his family were in earshot, but hoped he was getting the message. We lived on World's End Close, which was, without doubt, the dullest place on earth: a cul-de-sac of fourteen pairs of identical square white houses with net curtains at the windows and box-hedged gardens at their fronts. The garden at number two didn't quite count because no one had cut the grass there since old Mrs Patterson moved out in June. But the point was nothing ever happened round here. So, seeing a dead body might well be the single most exciting *and* terrifying moment of mine and Ray's lives.

Ray glanced down. 'What's with the coal bucket?'

'What? Oh!' I hadn't realised I was still carrying it. 'Never mind that. Can you—'

'Ray?' His mum interrupted from the sitting room. 'If that's Stevie, bring her inside.'

Unlike my family, Ray's used their sitting room every day: from it came the sound of dramatic, thumping music. They were lucky enough to have a television, and I often popped over to watch crime dramas and game shows, and a bit of *Blue Peter*.

'It's starting, Ray!' Mrs Johnson called again.

Ray's eyes flickered towards the sitting room: I'd lost his attention now, I could tell.

'President Kennedy's about to be on,' he said, beckoning me inside.

I hesitated. We had a dead body to inspect. Couldn't the news wait?

But Ray insisted. 'It'll only be a few minutes.'

Defeated, I put down the bucket. A few minutes at Ray's wouldn't make much difference. The body would still be dead. Yes, my mum would be wondering where the coal was, but the truth was I'd never win over President Kennedy, not in Ray's eyes: I knew better than to even try. Ray's mum was British, and his dad was African American, which meant Ray and his siblings had cousins on the other side of the Atlantic. When people looked at his skin colour and asked nosily if he spoke English, he'd say he was half-American, and proud of it. *So* proud he kept a scrapbook of cuttings from magazines and newspapers, and had written 'Important Americans' on the front.

After the cold of outside, Ray's sitting room felt deliciously warm. The curtains were drawn and the electric fire was on, the plastic logs glowing orange. All the Johnson family were there – Ray's parents, his sister Rachel and elder brother Pete, who did his hair in a rocker's quiff.

'Don't ever call me Elvis,' Pete warned anyone who tried. 'Ray Charles, Chuck Berry, Little Richard – they're the true kings of rock 'n' roll.'

As well as a television set, the Johnsons had a modern swirly brown carpet and a posh brown velvet settee that you weren't allowed to sit on if you were eating. Tonight, Ray's mum and sister had pulled it closer to the television.

'Hi,' I said to them all, ducking behind my fringe. Though I'd known Ray forever, I was still a bit shy around the Johnsons. It took me ages to get used to other people, and in a roomful of them, I tended to shrink into myself.

Pete lifted his chin at me in greeting. Rachel gave a little wave. Mr Johnson, Ray's dad, glanced up from the screen.

'Hey, Stevie, how're you doing? Fleabag not with you?' He loved dogs like I did, and said Flea was always welcome, even after the time she ate the bathroom soap, then sicked it up on the stairs.

'No,' I answered, then whispered to Ray as we squidged on to the settee, 'Promise we'll be quick?'

'It'll be minutes,' he assured me.

I folded my arms in my lap: I could probably sit still for that long.

On the TV, the intro music faded. The newsreader, with his immaculately parted hair and cut-glass accent, wished us all a good evening.

'Coming up, an announcement from the White House: we have a special report from our American correspondent . . .'

It was only now that I began to wonder what this 'special report' was about. Perhaps Mr Kennedy was sending another American up into space. Or sorting out the business in schools Ray had told me about, where his American cousins couldn't sit in the same classrooms as white kids or use the same toilets or restaurants. It must be important, whatever it was, because Ray's dad had come home early from the American airbase where he worked.

The scene then switched from the studio to America itself, and to a huge white building, flying the country's flag from its roof. A new voice – a woman's – came on air.

'Tension is mounting over Cuba . . .' the reporter said.

There was a brief shot of an island somewhere hot, then men in suits carrying important-looking files, then, at last, the President of the United States of America. He was sitting behind a desk, staring directly at the camera.

'Fellow Americans . . .' Mr Kennedy's square-jawed face filled the screen. Compared to our prime minister, who was old, with a droopy moustache, he looked film-star handsome.

The Cubans, Mr Kennedy told us, were building secret missiles. Russian ships were on their way across the ocean now, loaded with supplies to help make more of these weapons, which would be used to threaten America. This was why the American navy had blocked the Russian ships' route. Something like that, anyway. There was no mention of rights for black people or rockets going into space. It was all over very fast.

As the next news story began, I nudged Ray so he'd get to his feet too.

'Let's go,' I hissed, jerking my head towards the door.

He didn't move. The rest of the Johnsons all started talking at once.

'Where's Cuba?' Rachel wanted to know.

'On the other side of the world, baby, in the Caribbean,' Mr Johnson replied. 'It's a Communist country, so basically they're friends with the Russians.'

'It won't affect us, don't worry,' Mrs Johnson added.

'Yeah, but if the Cubans fire a nuclear missile at America and the Americans fight back, then – you heard him – they're only ninety miles off the American coast—' Pete mimed a big explosion with his hands.

'Whoa!' Rachel was startled. 'Is there going to be an actual war?'

Ray's parents shared a look, the sort adults did when you strayed too close to something they'd rather not talk about.

'How about I make some tea?' Mr Johnson said quickly.

Everyone moved off to the kitchen, except for Ray and me. We had more pressing matters to deal with.

*

When I told Ray what I'd found, I wasn't sure he believed me.

'A body? In your *shed*? Geez, Vie, are you sure?'

Which made me almost doubt it myself, especially once we were in the familiar surroundings of my back yard.

'Okay.' Ray squared his shoulders. 'Which shed is it in?'

We had two sheds – one for coal, the other for the washtub and mangle. Both were bolted shut.

'That one.' I pointed to the left-hand shed.

'Right.' Ray rubbed his palms over his clippered-short hair. It was a sure sign he was nervous, as was his tendency to talk a lot, which was what he then began to do.

'You're sure they're dead? How close did you get? Have you checked their pulse or anything? Did they have any belongings on them, like a wallet or a bus pass, because I think—'

'Ray?' I stopped him. 'When I looked, they weren't moving, all right? And before you ask, I've not told my mum yet, either.'

'Gee, okay. But how did anyone get in your shed in the first place? You reckon they weren't there earlier, when you got your bike out for your paper round?'

I shook my head. The paper round took about forty minutes. I did it every day, before and after school, and Flea came with me. But today she'd been a pest, barking at every cat we came across, so I'd taken her straight indoors when I got back, forgetting to put my bike away.

'The person must've turned up here after, what, half past three?' Ray pondered.

'I s'pose so.'

Though that didn't explain how they'd got into our back yard. To reach it you'd have to pass by the kitchen window, and Bev would've been home from school by then, making tea and toast like she did every night before starting her homework.

'The body?' I reminded him. 'Are we having a look or not? Because my mum'll be out in a minute, wondering where I am.'

Just as we inched forward, a noise came from the shed. A rumble as the coal moved. A bump. A scraping sound. Someone saying 'Ouch!' and 'Blast it!'

I looked at Ray: Ray looked at me.

The voice was a girl's, and she didn't sound dead in the slightest.

2

As Ray backed away from the door, I moved towards it.

'What should I do? Open it?' I hissed.

Ray pulled a worried face. 'I dunno, Vie. She might be an escaped criminal or a Russian spy, or … or … something.'

Though he had a point, he also had a wild imagination. It made him brilliantly clever at school in a way I could only dream of, though it wasn't much help to us right now. I was mulling over what to do next when I heard the back door of the house opening. Bright light and pop music tumbled out into the evening.

'Stevie?' my mum called, straining to see us from the doorstep. 'Hurry up, love. Have you gone to Newcastle for that coal?'

Luckily, I'd not yet switched my torch on again. All Mum would see of us was two dark shapes near the coal shed.

'Just a minute, Mum! Ray's here, I'm showing him

something on my bike,' I lied, and gave the pedal a clank with my foot for good measure.

'Get a move on, then. The boiler's almost cold and I want a bath.'

I held my breath till the back door closed again. We had minutes at most.

'I'm opening the shed,' I decided, picking up the bucket.

Ray came closer. 'I'm right behind you.'

'On the count of three . . . One . . . two . . .'

'Don't!' cried the voice from the other side of the door. 'I'll come out. We'll do this nicely. But you have to promise not to tell the police!'

My hand froze on the bolt. At my shoulder, Ray breathed in sharply.

'It locks from the outside. She can't get out,' I told him. 'We have to go in.'

Assuming the girl had heard me, I went in slowly. I expected her to be directly on the other side of the door, but she wasn't. I had to go further inside.

What struck me first was the odd smell – like soil, wet socks and ginger biscuits all mixed together. Something wispy brushed my face. Bev's bicycle handlebar jabbed me in the hip. Right behind me, so close I could feel him breathing on my neck, Ray tripped over the bike's pedal.

'Ouch! Where's the light switch?' he cried.

'There isn't one.' I rummaged for my torch and clicked it on.

This time I readied myself for the sight of a stranger's bobble hat. I shone my torch over the coal heap to the back of the shed where the biggest cobwebs lurked. There were spiders here, all right – plenty of them – but no sign of the girl.

Then, to my left, a shuffle.

I spun round. The girl slipped out from the space between the wall and the now open shed door. Her coat buttons glinted in the torchlight. She was wearing purple trousers, a huge black coat and the bobble hat, which was an unappealing green colour, rather like tinned spinach.

'Aarghh, not in my eyes!' She winced as the torchlight hit her face.

She had freckles, I noticed quickly, before lowering the beam. And she was probably about our age, though was far taller than anyone in our class at school. Now I wasn't blinding her, the girl stared straight at me. It wasn't a particularly friendly look, either. I took a wary step back.

'Who are you?' I asked.

The girl's chin wobbled a little. She looked away, blinking. Ray gave her a hankie from his pocket. As well as being better at the talking side of things, he knew how to be kind.

'Thanks.' The girl blew her nose, as loud as a trumpet.

'Keep it,' Ray said politely when she tried to give the hankie back to him. 'Can you tell us what you're doing here, please, because you're in my best friend's coal shed, and we don't know who you are.'

I'd never even *seen* the girl before, not at school or in the neighbourhood.

'You don't know who I am?' The girl seemed surprised. 'You mean, it's not been on the news?'

'About Cuba and the missiles?' Ray asked, but her shake of the head told us that wasn't what she meant.

'Oh, that's decent. *Very* decent.' The girl's shoulders slumped with relief, then under her breath, 'Maybe it *will* work if I'm careful.'

'What will?' I blurted out. 'And you still haven't said what you're doing here.'

The girl glanced from Ray to me and back again. Her face was beginning to soften.

'I've got to fetch something, that's all,' she said.

'What *something*?' I demanded.

Again, a look at me, at Ray. Underneath the cool act, she was still trying very hard not to cry.

'It's better I don't tell you,' she said firmly, sounding

quite posh and proper, unlike anyone else I knew. 'I'm sorry, all right? And I hate asking people for favours, but can I just hide here for tonight?'

Hide? This was getting more mysterious by the second.

Really, we should take her indoors, I thought. Get Mum to call the police. But Mum was about to have a bath, and though the girl wasn't giving much away, I couldn't help but feel sorry for her.

'I'll only be here for tonight, I promise,' the girl pleaded.

But what if Mum wanted more coal? What if Bev came outside, or Flea needed the toilet? What if they discovered I was hiding a stranger in our coal shed?

When I turned to Ray he shrugged his shoulders.

'Don't ask me,' he said. 'It's not my shed.'

Yet I knew that twinkly look of his. This wasn't the Ray Johnson who held doors open for teachers or did brilliantly well in spelling tests. This was the Ray who liked his adventures with a dash of mischief. It was one of the many reasons he was my best friend.

'Once this *something* turns up, you'll go?' I asked the girl.

'Tomorrow. Scout's honour.' She did the special Scout salute and gave us a sheepish grin, the cool act all but forgotten.

I nudged Ray. He nudged me back, which meant we were in agreement. What else would we be doing now, on a Tuesday evening? Nothing very interesting, probably. But a girl turning up out of nowhere – that *was* exciting. We'd be talking about it for weeks.

'Okay,' I agreed. 'But just for tonight.'

'We won't tell anyone we've seen you,' Ray assured her.

'Thanks. I mean it.' The girl sighed, smiled. 'What are your names, by the way?'

'Shouldn't *we* be the ones asking questions?' I muttered.

'I'm Ray Johnson,' Ray answered. 'And this is Stevie Fisher, who doesn't usually say very much, so you'll have to forgive her for being a bit *direct*.' He gave me a pointed look.

'My name's Anna,' the girl said. 'That's all you need to know. Just Anna.'

'Are you a criminal?' I wasn't trying to be funny, but she laughed – a big bright bark of a laugh that took me by surprise.

'Ha! I like that!'

Which I guessed meant she wasn't.

'What about your parents? Do they know you're here?' Ray asked.

Anna visibly twitched. 'Nope.'

Ray shot me a look, because our mums went spare if we weren't home by teatime.

'Are you a runaway, then?' I pressed her.

'I prefer to call it *taking charge of my own destiny*,' she said, rather grandly.

'Oh . . . um . . . okay.'

'And I know this sounds insane,' she added, 'but I'm probably being followed.'

'*What?* Who by?' Ray cried.

I groaned, wishing she'd told us this to begin with.

'Then I don't know if this is going to work—' I tried to say.

'Please, Stevie, let me stay till tomorrow,' she begged. 'Then I'll hit the road, Jack.'

'*Jack?*' I looked at her blankly.

'Like the song?' She started to sing it.

'It's by Ray Charles,' Ray explained, so I knew *he* was sold. 'Go on, it's only for one night, Vie.'

I wasn't honestly going to say no. Anna turning up had to be the most mysterious, intriguing thing to happen round here. And she needed help – *our* help – which made me realise just how rarely anyone else our age asked for it. Yes, at home Ray and me both did chores, but at school we were the girl who couldn't read very well and the boy whose mum married a man with different colour skin. The other kids skirted around us. We weren't part of things. Yet this strange girl was counting on us, which made me feel included, somehow.

'Just till tomorrow, then,' I said. 'And we'll try to bring you some food later too.'

Anna gave a long sigh of relief. 'Thank you.'

The coal had to come first, though. Hastily, I filled the bucket, and in the nick of time.

'Someone's coming!' Ray warned.

Anna ducked down. I switched off the torch. Everything went dark again – darker, after the light. Outside, the click-clack of heeled shoes crossed the yard towards us, and I heard Mum seething under her breath.

'Really, Stevie, you know I'm going away on my course tomorrow, and all I've asked you to do is—'

I barged out of the shed.

'I've got your coal,' I said, slightly breathless. 'I'd not forgotten.'

But I had forgotten about her trip away tomorrow, and that Nan was coming to look after us, which would make hiding Anna ten times harder.

3

Back in the kitchen, Mum was ironing her best blouses and explaining to Bev that, while she was away, there'd be no late nights, no parties, no missed schoolwork. And definitely no boyfriends. For once, I was grateful for their chatter and the pop music playing because it meant no one was paying attention to Ray and me.

'Boy*friend*, Mum,' Bev reminded her. 'I've only got the one.' He was called Gary, and was a Mod who rode a Lambretta scooter. When he came to ours, he'd fuss about getting dog hairs on his parka coat, which was probably why Flea always wanted to sit on him.

'You know exactly what I mean, miss,' Mum replied tartly.

'Well, if the Russians and Americans blow us up with nuclear weapons, you won't have to worry, will you?' Bev remarked.

I couldn't think about the missile business, not on top of everything else. Dumping the coal by the boiler,

I mouthed 'my room' to Ray. Upstairs we could talk in private, because if we were going to help Anna properly, then we needed a plan.

'Hang on, you two,' Mum said, noticing us sneaking off. 'Don't go upstairs – I'm about to have a bath.'

And she'd spend hours at it too, singing at the top of her voice, then wandering about afterwards in her dressing gown and curlers. The one consolation tonight was the lack of hot water: at least *this* bath would be a quick one.

'I'll get the Monopoly. Just act normal,' I whispered as Ray sat at the kitchen table.

I returned to find Bev pulling up a chair.

'You know Monopoly is awful, capitalist claptrap, don't you?' she said, but still wanted to play.

Bev was seventeen and went to the grammar school, and was always saying stuff I didn't understand. As well as brains, she had Dad's dark eyes, and wore her hair in a perfect 'Scooter Girl' bob. Half the boys at school were in love with her, much to her irritation.

As it was, I couldn't concentrate on Monopoly. Flea, who'd hopped up for a cuddle, sensed it and wouldn't sit still. Ray kept throwing terrible dice. Before long Bev was thrashing us both.

'That's fifty pounds rent, please,' she'd say literally

every time we moved our pieces. Little green plastic houses were popping up all over the board.

Then Ray ran out of money. He was, I realised, letting my sister win so the game would be over. And by a quarter to eight, it was. Mum, who'd finished her bath, called Bev upstairs – something about wanting a 'lucky' suitcase from on top of the wardrobe.

'Dad's old suitcase, that's what she means,' Bev said with a tut. It was another of Mum's little rituals that she always carried something of Dad's. Usually, it was his wedding ring that she wore on a chain around her neck. Or a brooch he'd given her, or one of his hankies stuffed in her pocket. Funny how she never wanted to talk about him, though.

Once Bev had gone upstairs, and Ray and me were finally alone, I leaned eagerly across the table.

'Who d'you think's following Anna?' I asked.

Ray considered it. 'Could be a friend. A sister. Someone she's fallen out with.'

'I thought she looked sad.'

'Yeah, and pretty determined.'

'She speaks like she's in the movies, doesn't she, even though she sounds posh.'

'She's just trying to be tough, I bet,' Ray replied.

'She didn't like asking for help, either, did she?'

'She's *in charge of her own destiny*, that's why.'

I frowned. 'What d'you reckon that means?'

'That she doesn't like being told what to do?'

I thought about it. 'But if she's being followed, why's she hanging around to collect something? If it was me I'd just run away.'

'Mysterious, isn't it?' Ray gave a little shiver. 'That's why it's so exciting!'

Upstairs, Mum and Bev were on the move again. We'd run out of time for coming up with a proper plan for Anna. But one thing I did know was how thin and hungry she looked. Quickly, I went to the pantry and took out bread, an apple, half a pork pie.

'What should I do to help?' Ray asked, watching me wrap the food in a tea towel.

'It's a cold night. She could do with a blanket.'

Ray got up. 'Sure. I'll fetch the spare one from my bed. Wait for me, won't you?'

I said I would. After all, we were in this together, and I wasn't quite feeling brave enough to face Anna on my own.

*

By bedtime, Ray still hadn't returned. His mum, I bet, had caught him smuggling a blanket out and got suspicious. It'd been too tricky to go outside again for me, too, what with Mum rushing about and Bev at the kitchen table, studying. In the end, I'd had to sneak the food package with me up to bed. Now my room smelled of pork pie.

I'd just switched off my bedside light when something hit my window. The noise came again, a *tick* against the glass. I sat up, alert. Someone was in the yard, throwing stones.

It had to be Ray.

I got dressed again, grabbed the food package, then listened at my door. Everyone else was in bed, the house so quiet and empty it felt strange as I tiptoed down the stairs. Times like this, I understood why Mum always kept the radio on: it stopped us listening out for Dad's voice.

Outside, someone tallish and short-haired in a zipped-up anorak was waiting by the shed. For a split second I wondered if it *was* Ray. Someone was following Anna: this might be him.

'Ray?' I whispered, anxious.

'Sorry I'm so late. My flipping brother decided to go to bed early!' Ray replied crossly. 'He's only just gone to sleep!'

I tried not to laugh. Poor Ray – he shared a bedroom with Pete, who went out most nights in his mate's car and stumbled home late, then got up very early in the morning for his job at the record shop in town. It was usually Ray needing more sleep, not the other way around.

As we opened the shed door, Anna scrambled to her feet.

'Hey, it's only us!' Ray winced, realising we'd startled her.

We gave Anna the blanket, which she wrapped around her shoulders, and the package of food. She devoured the pork pie and bread, cramming it into her mouth so fast she barely remembered to chew it.

'Thanks,' she said, wiping crumbs from her mouth when she'd finished. 'I needed that.'

She certainly looked better for eating something. To my surprise, she then said, 'Would you both stay a bit?'

'Ummm . . .' I glanced at Ray: he'd want to get home again, I guessed, and be fresh for school in the morning.

'Oh, go on,' Anna urged, brightening. 'Talk to me. Keep me company. Tell me who your favourite movie star is.'

'Sidney Poitier,' Ray said straight away. He had pictures of the actor in his 'Important Americans' scrapbook.

'Lassie,' I said, because it was the first thing that came into my head.

'Ha! Brilliant!' Anna did her big, loud laugh. 'Dogs and movies: my two favourite things in the world!'

'Our dog's called Flea and she's a pest. Though she's pretty sweet – if you like naughty dogs. Have *you* got a dog?' I asked, saying more to her than I ever did to the girls at school.

Anna's face closed. 'No questions about me, darned sorry and all that. The less you know, the less you'll be able to tell anyone.'

'I wouldn't say anything,' I replied, a bit taken aback. 'Not if I'd promised not to.'

'Stevie's totally honourable like that. You can trust us, you know,' Ray assured her.

Anna nodded, then, just like that, was all smiles again. 'I know, why don't we go for a walk?'

'*Now?*' Ray stared at her. 'But it's dangerous! You're being followed!'

'Not in the middle of the night, I won't be,' Anna replied with some confidence. 'And, no offence to your shed, Stevie, but all this sitting and waiting is doing my nut in. I need to take my mind off things.'

'Nah,' Ray insisted. 'It's not a good idea.'

'It's a totally *bonkers* idea,' I said. 'And it's ruddy freezing!'

*

Yet there we were, minutes later, walking across the waste ground behind my house. It had been farmland once, three huge, untidy fields that ran from the bottom of my garden all the way to the American airbase's perimeter fence. People said there was an old Second World War pillbox underneath the brambles in the furthest field, but we'd never found it, and Ray and me walked this route to school every day.

Recently, work had started to turn the first two fields into an estate of *executive* homes. The grass was now mud, the ground plotted out with pegs and string. And at night, with no streetlights and no residents yet, it felt strange and eerie. I kept close to Ray as we walked.

We weren't, I quickly realised, out here for a nice, chummy stroll. Anna walked very fast, with great, lolloping strides twice as long as ours. Soon she was a fair way ahead of us.

'This really isn't a good idea,' Ray muttered, blowing on his hands to warm them.

'You said yourself she doesn't like being told what to do,' I remarked.

'But she's not from round here,' he fretted. 'She doesn't

know the waste ground. She could break an ankle if she doesn't keep to the path.'

I was more concerned that we were being followed. It was deadly quiet out here, full of odd shapes and shadows. Every few steps, I'd stop, turn around and listen hard.

Which was how I lost sight of Anna, suddenly.

'Oh heck, where's she gone?'

'Off the path.' Ray's finger followed a person striding towards the airbase fence. 'Heading exactly where she *shouldn't* be going.'

I groaned.

Us local kids knew the American airbase was out of bounds. There were signs saying 'Keep Out' and 'Guards on Patrol', and rumours that an electric current ran through the fence. Ray's dad warned us about it countless times. Said the airbase authorities were very particular about 'prying' and 'snooping'. And there was Anna, heading right towards it.

We set off after her, running now.

'Anna!' Ray yelled. 'Don't touch the fence!'

The fence itself was still a few hundred yards away across the mud. But Anna, ahead of us, was only about twenty feet from it.

'Stop, Anna! The fence is electric!' I shouted.

I'd been scared enough watching the warning adverts they showed on television of what touching live electrics did: sparks. A flash. You'd be dead in an instant. Now, I could hardly breathe.

'Anna! You mustn't . . . out of bounds . . . !'

She was only a few feet from the fence. Her hands were out of her coat pockets.

'No!' Ray screamed.

Her arm was up. Her fingers were reaching. She spun around, bewildered, as if she'd only just remembered us. Her hand was on the chain-link fence.

The electricity was off.

I slowed to a walk, bent double in relief. Ray, though, charged right up to her.

'What are you doing?' he cried. 'It's an electric fence! Do you want to DIE?'

She actually *laughed*. 'Well, at least it would be quick and painless!'

'It's dangerous, Anna. We're not joking,' I warned.

'Keep your hair on. I'm all right, aren't I?' she said, surprised at our concern. 'What's so special about this place, anyway?'

We moved closer to the fence, this time being sure to stay together. Just beyond the boundary was the cracked concrete of an old, disused runway: from where we were standing, you couldn't see any buildings or aeroplanes. But all of it belonged to the American airbase. For training flights, the planes took off from the west runway on the other side of the hill: the old one hadn't been used since the last war.

'It's where the Americans keep their military aircraft,' Ray explained, calming down. 'Top secret and all that – which is why the fence is supposed to be live.'

From the direction of the runway, a light suddenly appeared.

We watched as the beam, strong as a headlight, came towards us. It had to be a car. Though it couldn't be, not from that direction. As the light got closer, it grew legs – four of them. Then voices, low and gruff, and the clanking of something metal being put down on the ground. The light was raised up, so it shone down on the concrete, revealing two men in overalls with paint tins and brushes.

Almost immediately, the men saw us.

'Hey!' the wider of the two men shouted. 'You shouldn't be here!'

The light swooped towards us, so dazzling I had to shield my eyes.

'Kids! I might have known.' The wide man swaggered towards the fence. 'The electricity's going back on tonight, I'm warning you. Five hundred volts down your arm and you won't be back in a hurry.'

*

In the safety of my coal shed again, we talked anxiously about what we'd seen.

'Those men were painting something, weren't they?' I said.

Anna nodded. 'Lines on the runway, by the look of it.'

'Geez, they must be about to start using it again,' Ray replied, rubbing his head. 'Just in case—'

'– there's another war,' I finished.

In all the time I'd lived here, I'd never seen a plane take off from the old runway. America and the Soviet Union had been enemies for years. People called it the Cold War because no fighting ever took place. It was just men in suits giving angry speeches about the other side. On the news, though, President Kennedy had said he'd protect America at all costs. Their planes were here at the airbase – American jets loaded with American bombs – all within striking distance of Russia.

I caught myself thinking of Dad, suddenly. He rarely talked about his time in the army, but there was one thing he did mention: it sent a chill through my bones.

'If there is another world war,' he said, 'mark my words, it'll be our last.'

Day Two

RUSSIAN SHIPS BOUND FOR CUBA TOLD: RETURN HOME OR FACE CONSEQUENCES

The Daily Times, Wednesday 24 October 1962

4

I was rubbish at getting up for my paper round. Usually, it took three alarm clocks, and Mum yelling up the stairs, 'Stevie, have you *died*?' to stir me in the morning. Today, I was wide awake before the first alarm, the flutter in my stomach reminding me something had happened.

Anna.

I sat up, hugging my knees to my chest. Last night's adventures felt less thrilling this morning, a bit like being left with the washing-up after a birthday party. We were hiding a girl we barely knew in my coal shed – a girl who was being followed.

What if Mum found out? What if the police got involved? What if the people following Anna had already seized her in the night?

Thinking I'd better check, I went to the window and parted the curtains. It was beginning to get light outside. Our back yard looked reassuringly normal: frosty cobbles, our washing line with the peg bag hooked over it, a blackbird on the wall, singing. The shed door was closed, just as we'd left it last night. Anna, I figured, was probably still down there, so I'd be able to double check she was leaving today like she promised, and get the chance to say a proper goodbye.

Someone else was up early too. Down in the kitchen the kettle whistled, cupboard doors opened, the radio burbled on. Grabbing my school uniform from the chair, I got dressed and tied my hair in a ponytail. In the dressing-table mirror I was still the same plain, mousy girl, hiding behind her fringe. No one would know, just from looking at me, that I was keeping such a gigantic secret.

Downstairs, Mum's suitcase stood packed and ready in the hallway. Again, it'd slipped my mind that she was going away today. All the way up to Liverpool on a course for her job at the huge, modern hospital in town. She'd told us about it a couple of weeks ago.

'Conflict resolution, that's what they're training us in,' Mum explained.

I'd had to ask Bev what 'conflict resolution' meant.

'It's so people can make up again after they've had a slanging match,' she said.

'Like a referee?'

'Yes.' Bev laughed. 'A referee between the doctors and nurses.'

Mum wouldn't be back till Saturday, so Nan was coming to look after us – the last resort, Bev called it, because although Mum and Nan didn't get on, we had no other family to ask. Nan was Dad's mother, and liked to talk about how brave he'd been in the army, which made Mum upset.

Yet part of me was glad Nan was coming. We'd not seen her for ages, even though she didn't live far away in one of the new council flats in town. I missed talking about our dad with someone who'd known him. There was a downside to Nan, though. She was as nosy as anything, so it was a good job Anna would be gone by the time she arrived.

In the kitchen, Mum was at the table, stirring her tea. She was wearing lipstick and her smart coat with the furry collar; on it she'd pinned her four-leaf clover brooch, a birthday present from Dad. I couldn't remember the last time I'd seen her so dressed up.

'You look nice,' I told her, sitting down.

Flea, hopping out of her bed, came over and licked my knee.

'Ta, love.' Mum frowned at me over her teacup. 'You're up early, aren't you?'

'I couldn't sleep.'

Mum gave my shoulder a fond squeeze, which, since

she wasn't normally a cuddly, kissy sort of mum, felt nice. She then got up from the table.

'Help yourself to my breakfast,' she said. 'I overdid it, rather.'

The toast rack was full of hot toast, the teapot steamed. A couple of boiled eggs, one with the top already sliced off, looked perfect for dipping soldiers into. There was easily enough here for two – me and Anna. As I tucked in, I made sure to keep back half of everything, to take out to the shed.

Mum, meanwhile, was watching at the window.

'My taxi'll be here any minute. You'll be all right, you and Bev, won't you? I'll only be gone a few days.'

She was nervous about leaving us, I realised. Even the cheery pop song on the radio couldn't cover it.

''Course,' I answered, my mouth full of egg. 'I might even get to the paper shop on time this morning!'

Mum turned to me, a wistful look on her face. 'Oh, Vie, your dad always said you were a hard worker.'

I lowered my spoon. It was the first time, I was sure of it, that she'd mentioned Dad in months. Maybe it was because she was going away on a work trip, like Dad often did in his army days.

On his last trip before he got sick, he came home with the most incredible suntan and told us what hard work it had been, lying on a beach for two months. He was joking, I knew, but he never did tell us what he'd really been up to. Bev said Mum and Nan had different opinions on the subject. That was another reason why they didn't get along.

'Did Dad really say that?' I asked now.

'He did.' Mum briefly touched the brooch on her lapel. 'He was the same – for what good it did him.'

I wasn't sure what she meant, and was about to say so when a car pulled up outside, beeping its horn. Mum checked at the window.

'That's my taxi. I'm travelling in style today!'

She laughed, excited now as well as nervous, batting me away as I got up to hug her goodbye.

'Best not, there's a dear. You'll crush my outfit,' she said, and hurried out into the hall for her suitcase. Her head appeared round the door one final time. 'Your nan'll be here later to keep an eye on you. Sure you'll be all right?'

'We'll be fine,' I promised, though I'd have felt better if she'd given me that hug.

*

Out in the back yard, the sky was brightening. Flea, skittering over the icy cobbles, made a beeline for the shed. She scratched at the door, whimpering to be let in.

'Hold your horses,' I muttered, because I was trying to knock and carry tea and toast for Anna at the same time.

No one answered, so I opened the door with my foot. I felt suddenly shy about seeing Anna again. Flea, who had no such qualms, shot past my legs, tail wagging.

'Oi!' I hissed. 'Come back!'

A typical terrier, Flea ignored me, scrambling over the coal until she found what I guessed was Anna. I couldn't see much, just my dog's tail wagging madly.

'Oh, hello *you*,' Anna crooned, her voice thick and sleepy. 'Aren't *you* a little poppet?'

'I've brought you some breakfast,' I said.

Resting the teacup on the window ledge, I balanced the toast on top and told Flea again to come. Finally, smelling food, she did.

'What time is it?' Anna sat up. She was still wearing the sludge-green bobble hat.

'Quarter to seven.'

'Okay, early, then.' She lay back under Ray's blanket, pulled it up to her chin and closed her eyes. It was what Bev did when she wanted me out of her bedroom: she'd pretend to be asleep so I'd go away.

I hovered, nervously.

'You will be leaving today, won't you?' I said, because I needed to be sure.

'Said I would, didn't I?' Anna replied, not opening her eyes. 'No need to be unfriendly.'

'I wasn't!' I flustered. Ray was so much better at talking to people than I was. 'I just meant have you got somewhere else to go?'

'Yes, I'll be fine.'

'Only my nan's coming to stay, and she—'

'Listen, Stevie.' Anna propped herself up on an elbow to look at me. She was pale this morning, dark under the eyes. 'Don't worry, I'll be out of your hair today.' She did the three-fingered Scout sign again and pulled a goofy face.

'I'm being serious,' I insisted. 'The thing you're collecting—'

'Havana Road,' she interrupted. 'That's near here, isn't it?'

'Errr . . . yes . . . it's the main road up by the shops.' I hesitated. 'Why, what are you picking up?'

She lay back, closing her eyes again. 'No questions, remember?'

And that was how we left it – Anna going back to sleep, and me supposing I'd never see her again.

*

It was later than I thought. Out in the close, the frost on people's front lawns was melting in the early sunshine. Bottles of milk stood breakfast-ready on doorsteps, a sign the milkman had already been. Curtains in front rooms were opening, the smell of burnt toast filled the air. It wouldn't be long before people realised their papers hadn't arrived. This morning, like all others, Flea came with me on my round. It'd taken a lot of bacon rinds to train her to trot alongside my bike, but she was usually fine now, as long as we didn't see any cats, like we did yesterday. Or big white dogs: for some reason, she hated those.

Cycling up the road, I noticed the front gate to number two was open. Ever since Mrs Patterson had gone to live with her daughter, the house had been empty. A 'To Rent' sign had been up for ages, but no one seemed interested in living there. Over the summer the garden had grown into a jungle of grass and nettles, but today a man in overalls was finally cutting it all back.

I was too concerned about being late to pay much attention. Mr Talbot, who owned the paper shop, said he knew at least ten other kids who'd give their back teeth for a round like mine, where the houses were close together and the dogs too lazy to bark. The paper round even ended here in World's End Close: three *News of the Worlds*, a *Daily Mirror* for Ray's parents, a *Telegraph* for Mrs Baldwin at number five. Bev reckoned you could tell a lot about a person by what newspaper they read.

Mr Talbot was outside the shop, waiting, when I arrived. I screeched to a halt, narrowly missing his foot. Flea, the little traitor, wagged her tail at him.

'Ten past seven,' Mr Talbot stated, tapping his wristwatch. 'You're twenty minutes late, Stephanie.'

He never called me Stevie. In the last war, he'd served in the army just like my dad and Ray's. He insisted the most important thing the army taught him was time-keeping, and that I had a lot to learn on this matter.

'Sorry, Mr Talbot.' He never believed my excuses anyway, so I usually just made something up. 'I got stuck in a—'

'What was it this time, I wonder?' he interrupted. 'A space ship? A time warp?'

I waited patiently for him to finish. The truth was, I needed this job. Mum wouldn't be happy if I got the push. She was a firm believer in Bev and me paying our way, and had begged Mr Talbot to take me on in the first place, even though he thought paper rounds were for boys.

'… so you leave me with no other option,' Mr Talbot was saying now, 'than to give you a final warning.'

I felt my jaw drop. This was serious.

'I mean it,' he insisted, as if it hadn't registered on my face. 'Next time you're late, I'll have to let you go.'

'It won't happen again,' I promised.

'Good.' Mr Talbot patted Flea. 'How's the little one today?'

I'd always suspected he liked my dog far more than he liked me. Leaving him and my bike outside, I hurried inside to fetch the newspapers.

'Better late than never,' Mrs Talbot remarked from her spot behind the counter, half hidden by a wall of tinned fish and shoe polish.

She handed me my delivery bag with an irritable sigh. It felt heavier than usual. When a big story broke, suddenly everyone wanted their own newspaper: last time was when that American actress, Marilyn Monroe, died. This time, I guessed, it was Cuba and its secret missiles.

'The Americans and Russians are at it again,' Mrs Talbot confirmed, holding up the *Daily Mirror* she'd been reading.

The headline said: 'US HUNTS TARGET …' I couldn't read the last part.

'It's getting serious,' Mrs Talbot said with an ominous

raise of the eyebrows. 'Those Commies in Cuba building missiles with the Russians' help, and us on the American side, with their airbases on our soil and whatnot. If there's a war, we'll all get dragged in.'

I gulped miserably. The men we'd seen last night, painting lines on the old runway, were preparing for war, weren't they?

'Of course, everyone's worried they'll use nuclear bombs,' Mrs Talbot added. 'Like they did against the Japanese—'

The shop darkened as Mr Talbot came inside.

'Now, now, Jean,' he said. 'Don't frighten the child.'

It was a bit late for that. Though I was too young to remember the last war, I'd seen pictures – of Dad and Mr Johnson in their army uniforms, Mum as a Wren, her hair in sausage curls. All of them smiling for the camera, all being brave.

One particular photograph came to mind now. It was on the wall of Ray's living room and showed Mrs Johnson on a beach with a lighthouse in the background. Ray said it was taken in Devon, where his mum grew up, and where she'd met his dad when he'd been stationed there. It was also where the Johnsons went on holiday every summer.

This particular photo wasn't a holiday snap, though.

It was of Mrs Johnson – Queenie – as a young woman. Even then she wore glasses and terrible sweaters, and didn't smile much. During the war, she'd helped Jewish refugees fleeing Hitler. She broke the law to do it, Ray told me, but she saved those people's lives. Nowadays, to me, she was Ray's mum, the person who called him in for his tea and made sure he'd done his homework. It was easy to forget that she'd been someone else once – that she'd had to be.

But that was what wars did: they changed people and they changed the world. Only this war, over Cuba's missiles, would be different, because if what Dad said was true then it would change our world forever, wouldn't it, by ending it.

5

At eight o'clock on the dot, Ray called round for school. I was bursting to talk to him about last night at the airbase, about Anna leaving. But he stopped me before I'd even got my anorak on.

'Sorry, Vie,' he said. I realised what he meant when I saw his sister Rachel, waiting for us on the pavement.

'Great,' I muttered under my breath.

'Layla's poorly, so Mum says I'm to walk with you today.' Rachel beamed, because she loved any excuse to hang out with us.

'Yeah, and she'll be better tomorrow,' Ray reminded her, firmly.

Normally it wouldn't have mattered. But it was just our luck, now we had an important secret to discuss, that Rachel was in tow. We'd have to wait until break time to talk about Anna.

As it was, Rachel didn't stop chattering the whole way to school. She wanted to be an actress when she was older – 'A famous one, like in Hollywood' – and was auditioning for a part in the school Christmas play. She already knew all the lines off by heart.

'Go on, test me,' she begged.

By the time we got to school, we'd gone through them so many times, I could've played the part myself.

*

When the bell went for break, Ray and I fetched our milk and hurried outside. Leaning against the playground wall, we watched the other kids play a scrappy game of Bulldog.

'Anna was still there this morning,' I told Ray. 'I took her some breakfast.'

'Was she okay? Any signs of anyone else snooping about?'

'No, only Flea, who wouldn't stop licking her.'

'Ugh, grim.' Ray pulled a face; he wasn't especially fond of dogs. 'She's still leaving later, isn't she? That's still happening?'

'She has to. She can't hide in our shed forever.'

Ray took a slurp of milk, thinking. 'I wish she could, though. Just for a bit longer. It's exciting having her around.'

'Hmmm, I know what you mean.'

'Last night at the airbase was a proper little adventure, wasn't it?'

I grinned. 'Just a bit!'

The fact was I couldn't remember the last time we'd done anything so daring. But what we'd seen up there still bothered me.

'D'you think there will be a war?' I asked. 'Because Mrs Talbot at the paper shop thinks the whole WORLD is about to end.'

I'd meant it as a sort of nervous joke, but Ray didn't smile.

'President Kennedy can't just stand back and let the enemy win, Stevie. Remember, he's not the one building missiles.'

Only because he probably had plenty of his own already, I thought grimly.

Still, there was no point arguing with Ray over America. So I drank my milk, which had been sitting on a windowsill in the sunshine and tasted warm and clotted, then went back to the subject of Anna.

'I wonder what she's going to collect today and why it's so important,' I mused.

'Or where she's getting it from,' Ray added.

'She did ask where Havana Road was,' I remembered.

'S'pose she might've needed to go to the Co-op. Did you ask her?'

'I tried: *no questions* – that's what she said. Like I was pestering her. But my nan's coming later, that's why Anna needs to be gone.'

'Holy moly! Your *nan*!' Ray rolled his eyes.

Because if anyone could sniff out the girl hiding in our coal shed, I'd put money on it being my grandmother.

*

The rest of the day was slow torture, sitting through lessons, wondering about Anna. I'd daydream I was with her, walking to Havana Road, or waving her off like a proper friend at the station. In reading time, I was clumsier than ever: Miss Elliott, our nice teacher who usually encouraged me, looked concerned as I stumbled over the words.

Once the final lesson was over, Ray and me ran straight home. We found the shed door wide open. My bike was where I'd left it that morning, propped against the wall of the house. And next to it, on the ground, was the teacup – now empty – that I'd brought Anna at breakfast. Everything was quiet.

'She's gone.' I breathed out, feeling my shoulders unknot.

'Looks like it.'

Ray was disappointed, I could tell.

'Ah well, it must've worked out all right, fetching whatever it was,' I reasoned.

But after the first wave of relief, I felt rather flat. I wasn't ready for our adventure to be over either.

Meanwhile, I had an evening paper round to do. With Mr Talbot's warning about punctuality still ringing in my ears, I went indoors to fetch Flea. She came flying out to greet us like a hairy whirlwind.

'Whoa!' Ray jumped back, hands in the air. 'What's the matter with your dog?'

'She's missing Mum, I expect.'

I clipped on Flea's lead, telling her to stop her nonsense. But as I wheeled my bike out to the front gate, she kept leaping about and trying to nibble our ankles, and generally being a pain. In the end, Ray suggested he'd take her for a walk, instead.

'You?' I didn't mean to sound ungrateful, but he'd never offered before.

'Sure. Why not?'

I could think of several reasons, including the fact that today she was being particularly mad. But I couldn't risk being late for work again.

'Thanks ever so.' I handed over the lead. 'If you're going to the waste ground, don't let her off. You know what she's like when she sees a cat. And if you see another dog, she's scared of them, so just walk away. I'll be back as quick as I can.'

*

Thirty minutes of rolling up papers, pushing them through letter boxes and I finished in record time. I half expected Ray and Flea to still be out when I got home. Instead, Ray was waiting in our kitchen. Alone. One look at his face, and I knew something was wrong.

'Where's Flea?' I asked, worried now.

Ray was starting to explain when Bev appeared, carrying Flea wrapped in a towel.

'She's fine,' Bev tried to reassure me. 'It was only a nip. I couldn't find the antiseptic to put on it, but I've washed off most of the blood.'

'Blood? Where?' I took Flea from her, opening the towel.

Her white fur was stained rusty red from her shoulder right down to her paw. Our poor little dog looked so sorry for herself, I started to cry.

'Who did this?' I sobbed.

'Another dog,' Ray said.

'Whose *dog*?' I demanded, my voice rising.

'I don't know. I didn't recognise it. It came out of nowhere, Vie.' Ray was gabbling, like he always did when he was nervous. 'And Flea was going ballistic. The dog was a white one, did I say that? It was running around off its lead and trying to—'

'I told you to keep her on her lead!' I interrupted. 'And I warned you about other dogs!'

'Stevie.' Bev reasoned. 'Flea was on her lead. Don't blame Ray. It was an accident. It's only a little bite. It looks worse than it is. She'll be fine.'

'I'm sorry, Stevie. I did my best,' Ray said, looking close to tears himself.

I turned away. It wasn't his fault, I knew that really: these things happened, especially with terriers. But I was upset. I wanted to know who this white dog belonged to, so I could give them a piece of my mind.

*

'Don't be mad with Ray,' Bev said, once he'd gone. 'He's a good friend to you, that one. Flea'll be all right.'

'It's that white dog's owner I'm mad at, not Ray,' I replied.

We sat in silence. No one had turned the radio on yet or started making tea. Without Mum our normally warm, noisy kitchen felt a bit too quiet. I shivered, and nuzzled Flea's neck.

'Oh, Stevie, Flea'll be fine,' Bev tried to reassure me again.

'So you keep saying,' I snapped.

Bev's mouth tightened. 'For goodness' sake, there's about to be a nuclear war and all you're worried about is a silly dog bite!'

'It's not silly to me! And shut up about the stupid war!'

'Not likely!' Bev answered. 'You can sit around waiting for it to happen. But I'm going to do my bit and make the government listen.'

With an almighty huff, she started yanking books from her school bag and dumping them on the table. I'd had enough, and stomped upstairs. I was crying again. I missed Mum. She'd know where the antiseptic was, to put on Flea's shoulder. But when I climbed on a chair to look inside the bathroom cabinet, all I could find were corn plasters and chilblain cream.

Giving up, I went to my room and lay on the bed, still cuddling Flea. I remembered the day she'd arrived as a puppy. It was just before Dad got sick. He'd brought her home from the allotment in the same bag as all the fresh beans and potatoes he'd grown.

'. . . and not just spuds,' Dad said, holding the bag open so I could peep inside. 'We've been growing puppies on the allotment, as well.'

To start with, Flea was as tiny as a guinea pig. I had to feed her milk every few hours, then, as she got bigger, mashed lamb and porridge from the end of my finger. She was such a naughty, clever little dog. She knew exactly how to make me laugh. But as Flea grew fatter, Dad seemed to get thinner, until he could hardly climb the stairs without coughing. I often wondered if he already knew how sick he was when he brought Flea home, because having a dog made the hard times a bit more bearable.

But tonight, I was hurting and Flea wasn't helping much. I kept thinking about the war, and what Dad had said, and how when someone important went away, they left an empty feeling in your chest. First Dad, then Mum, now Anna: they'd all gone.

Life in World's End Close would go back to normal, the daily, dull-as-double-maths plod of paper rounds, school, tea, homework. I'd be the same Stevie Fisher, too shy to take charge of anything much, never mind her own destiny. At least, things might've been that way, before I met Anna. But that old life didn't seem enough any more.

6

The doorbell rang three times in quick succession. It was typical of Nan not to push the bell once and wait.

'No! Don't jump!' I winced as Flea leaped off the bed and ran downstairs, totally oblivious to her bite wound. Racing after her, I managing to scoop her up before opening the front door.

Nan was on the doorstep with a suitcase at her feet.

'Thought you hadn't heard me,' she said, shouldering her way inside.

'Fat chance of that,' Bev muttered, joining us in the hallway. She shot me a quick smile to show she wasn't cross any more. I smiled back, relieved.

'Cheeky as ever, I see, Beverley,' Nan remarked. 'And to think I missed my darts night to come and look after you two.'

'I'm *joking*, Nan.' Bev sounded exasperated already. 'Here, let me take your coat.'

Though I'd known her all my life, Nan's outfits still

surprised me. She had a knack for wearing patterns that clashed so badly my eyes got confused just from looking at her. Tonight's get-up – a leopard-print coat with a red paisley headscarf – was actually quite tame, and I was glad. All that crying earlier had given me a headache.

In the kitchen, Bev had set three places at the table. The boiler was warm, the curtains drawn, the radio blaring out a pop song. Bev was wearing Mum's orange apron with 'Home Sweet Home' written on the bib. She was trying to keep everything normal, and I felt so grateful I almost welled up again.

'What's for tea?' Nan asked.

'Toast and omelette,' Bev replied.

'Not a proper cooked meal, then?' Nan opened cupboard doors, shutting them with a disappointed tut. 'Ah, I see. Your mother's not been to the shops.'

'It's been a bit of an evening, Nan,' Bev explained, then told her about Flea.

Nan was horrified. 'Fancy letting a vicious dog roam about like that. I've a good mind to speak to the owners.'

'That's just it, we don't know who the owner is,' I pointed out.

'She's looking better now, though, isn't she?' Bev said,

as we watched Flea limp around the kitchen, sniffing for crumbs.

I agreed she was. Certainly, the sight of our little hairy dog with dried blood on her shoulder seemed to soften Nan. As Bev got on with cooking tea, Nan sat down with Flea on her lap and hand-fed her corned beef from a tin she found at the back of the larder. I hardly noticed the news come on the radio, though Nan did, her head whipping round like a shot.

'Switch it off, Bev,' she ordered.

'But we always—'

'Switch it off!' Nan insisted.

With a sulky huff, Bev clicked off the radio.

'This ruddy missile business,' Nan tutted. 'Gets on my nerves. To think your poor dad fought Hitler for us to listen to squabbles like this.'

'He wouldn't want another war, would he?' I asked, glad we were already talking about Dad.

Nan looked a bit surprised. 'If he was in the army still, he'd do what he had to. He was loyal to his country.'

At the stove, Bev turned around.

'What's the point? No one could win a nuclear war,' she said.

Nan puffed out her chest. 'Ah, see, this is where me and your mother disagree. I say, if having those bombs means everyone's too scared to use them, then that's good, isn't it?'

'No, it's not, Nan,' Bev hit back. 'All it takes is one power-hungry person to push a button . . .'

Nan wafted the idea away. 'These politicians, they're like kids fighting over a football. It's all just bluff and posturing. They'll calm down eventually.'

'Or *we* can do something about it ourselves.'

Bev showed us the badge she was wearing on her school jumper. I'd not noticed it earlier. The symbol looked like an upside-down Y with three arms.

'I've joined the Campaign for Nuclear Disarmament – CND,' she explained proudly.

Nan's eyebrows went skyward. 'You've not gone all *political*? Lordy, Bev, you'll be turning into one of those vegetarians next!'

I caught Bev's eye and tried not to smile.

'What does your young fella make of it – Gary, isn't it?' Nan went on. 'The lad with the scooter?'

'He's not my fella any more. He didn't think much of me joining CND, so I gave him the elbow.'

I didn't know this; nor did Nan. 'Oh, who's the lucky boy now, then?'

'No one,' Bev replied. Though as she started beating eggs again, I swore there was a blush creeping up her neck.

*

After tea, just as I was summoning up the courage to go to Ray's, Nan insisted we sort out our sleeping arrangements.

'I suppose you all cram into one room upstairs, as well?' she sniffed.

The remark came after she'd tried to take her evening cuppa into the parlour.

'Don't!' Bev had cried, as Nan went to open the always closed door. 'It's not . . . I mean . . . we don't go in there.'

'Why ever not?' Nan asked.

Bev didn't know. Nor did I. Our kitchen was the noisy hub of the house, and I didn't think to question it. When Dad was alive we'd used the parlour most evenings, but these days we kept it as spotless as a museum.

Upstairs were two bedrooms: Bev and Mum's at the front, which was the biggest, with twin beds, and my tiny box room at the back.

'You'll sleep in Mum's bed, won't you?' I asked Nan.

It made sense that she would: the front room was prettier, with net curtains at the window and flowery eiderdowns. Admittedly, Bev had stuck music posters all around her bed – the Beatles, the Kinks, and bands

I didn't know – but surely Nan would prefer that to my room, which smelled of dog and, still faintly, of pork pie.

'Oh no!' Nan said, like I was mad to suggest it. 'I can't share a room with anyone, Stevie. Not with my *difficulties*.'

My heart sank: she'd set her sights on *my* room. Bev wasn't happy, either. She'd always hated sharing a bedroom with me. We used to have bunk beds – Bev in the top bunk, of course. But she'd always complained that I snored like a creaking ship, which was why, these days, she shared with Mum.

'Nan, please,' I begged. 'Bev won't want to share with me.'

'She won't want me in with her, either,' Nan pointed out. 'Especially if I've eaten eggs, or cabbage. It plays havoc with my—'

'All right,' Bev interrupted. 'We get the message.'

So it was me who had to move. And as I did so I thanked my lucky stars that Anna wasn't still out in the coal shed, just feet away beneath my bedroom window. In her room, Bev suggested we shift the big wardrobe so it stood between our beds like a dividing wall.

'Anything to dull the noise,' she explained.

I'd already resigned myself to nights of her throwing

pillows at me and yelling 'STOP SNORING', so this struck me as one of Bev's better ideas. Still, it was a hefty wardrobe to shift. It'd belonged to Nan's parents – Dad's grandparents. It was solid oak, with a long mirror on the front, and was stuffed full of Mum and Bev's clothes. On top were a few dusty hat boxes and the suitcase Mum hadn't taken to Liverpool.

'Leave them. They won't fall off,' Bev said, as I reached to take everything down.

Between us, we wriggled the wardrobe away from the wall and across the floor. It was hard, thumping work. Bev was on the other side, pressed against the mirrored part.

'One more push,' she panted.

As the wardrobe lurched, everything on top started sliding towards me. I tried to fend off the boxes, the lids, the old suitcase tumbling down. Something hit my shoulder, a shoe bounced off my head. The rest landed on the bed I was meant to be sleeping in, covering everything in dust and cobwebs.

'Great,' I muttered.

Then Nan shouted from downstairs – I didn't hear what, but Bev did, being nearer the bedroom door.

'Let her out if she needs the loo, Nan,' she called, then to me, 'She's worrying over the dog, *again*.'

'I'll do it,' I said, because Flea was my responsibility, and I'd had enough of moving furniture.

*

Outside, Flea made a beeline for the coal shed.

'You're here for a wee, not to chase rats,' I warned her, picking her up before she could injure herself any more.

Flea scrabbled to get down again.

'Stop it, you—' I froze.

Something moved inside the shed. It wasn't quick enough to be a rat. And rats didn't do big, heavy sighs, either. I inched open the door.

'Anna?' I whispered, heart thumping. 'Is that *you*?'

7

She was sitting on the coal heap in a patch of moonlight.

'What're you doing here?' I asked, astonished.

'This isn't how it looks, I promise.' Anna tried to get up, but lost her footing. She sat down heavily, thumping the coal in frustration.

Something had gone wrong today, that was obvious. Even Flea knew not to go to Anna right then, and kept very still, tucked under my arm. I pulled the door shut behind me. The shed felt tiny, suddenly: damp, cobwebby, all dark shapes and suspicion. But better that than someone hearing us.

'I didn't mean to come back,' Anna said.

The wobble was there in her voice again. Her trousers were ripped at the knee. She'd pulled her hat down low, so it was hard to see her eyes. Ray would have known what to say, but I felt tongue-tied and flustered.

'The thing you were meant to collect—' I started.

'– wasn't where it should've been,' she finished. 'I had it all planned out, didn't I, then I messed up.'

'How?'

Anna took a long breath.

'I'm going to tell you this much because you and Ray, you've been a big help to me.'

Despite how weird this all was, I smiled. 'It's been fun having you here.'

'No, Stevie, this isn't fun. The people following me are trying to poison me.' She said it slowly, clearly, but it didn't sink in.

'Poison.' I repeated it back, trying to understand. 'Someone wants to *poison* you?'

'Yes. With arsenic.'

I waited for her to laugh. Or say it was just a joke, or the plot of one of those dark, twisty films she probably loved, where the actors wore trilby hats and smoked cigarettes under streetlights.

But she didn't.

Fear hit me square in the chest.

'Crikey, Anna, then they're almost murderers!' I gasped. 'We have to tell the police!'

She stiffened. 'No! That's exactly what they want to happen! We'd be playing straight into their hands.'

But I was scared. How did we know these poisoners

weren't already spying on my house or Ray's? I could almost picture them, a pair of men in mackintoshes, their binoculars trained on the coal shed. At Ray's we often watched a police TV show called *Z-Cars*, so I knew a bit about criminals. If someone wanted to kill Anna, we'd never be able to hide her for long.

'We're friends, aren't we, Stevie?' Anna asked.

I'd already counted her as a friend, to be honest, but was very glad she'd said it too.

'We are.' I nodded firmly.

'Then let me stay a few more days,' Anna pleaded.

I stared at her.

It wouldn't work, not for that length of time, keeping her hidden from Nan, sneaking out food, making sure no one poisoned her.

'The … the … shed doesn't lock,' I stuttered. 'It's not safe.'

'It's safer here than anywhere else.'

'But someone might sneak down the alley or over the back hedge – we did it ourselves last night,' I reminded her. 'And my nan's sleeping in my bedroom and the window looks down on the yard. She's bound to see you.'

'Please, just till the end of the week. I'll try and get him again then. I wouldn't ask if I wasn't desperate.'

'*Him?*' I pressed. 'So it's a person you're collecting, not a thing?'

The question made her bite her lip.

I sighed. I wanted to help her, and be the friend she said I was. She didn't seem to have anyone else to turn to. But could we really keep her safe in our coal shed?

'Let me think a minute,' I muttered, wishing Ray was here because he'd have known what to do.

Anna tugged at her bobble hat. The movement caught Flea's attention: all this time she'd been quietly tucked under my arm, but now she pawed Anna's leg.

'Mind if I hold her?' Anna asked.

'Sure.' I knew from experience that hugging a dog often helped when you felt upset. 'Just be careful, though. She got bitten today on her shoulder – it's the left side.'

Anna took Flea gently, and placed her on her lap. 'Poor little girl, you're hurt, are you?'

'She probably annoyed the other dog,' I admitted. 'Flea can be a bit snappy.'

'Don't blame your dog. I bet it was the owner's fault, the stupid fool.'

I shrugged. 'Maybe. It was Ray walking her, not me. He didn't recognise the other dog – a big white one, apparently.'

'*White?*' A strange look flickered over Anna's face.

‘Yup. And no sign of the owner.’

‘Oh well,’ she said a bit too briskly.

She started rummaging through the duffel bag at her feet. Clothes, books, a half-eaten packet of ginger biscuits and what looked like a sponge bag spilled out. It was this she grabbed with a satisfied ‘Ah!’ and took out a glass jar.

‘Antiseptic,’ she said, giving the jar to me. ‘For Flea’s shoulder. I’d do more if I could. I owe you and Ray.’

‘Thanks, but we wanted to help,’ I insisted. ‘Maybe *fun* isn’t the right word for it but, honestly, life in World’s End Close was so boring before you came along.’

Despite everything, Anna smiled.

‘Well, then,’ she said.

I found myself smiling back. And again, I thought how different she was from the girls in my class at school, who wore their hair in perfect pigtails and talked behind their hands. In all the years I’d known them, they’d never wanted to be pals. Yet here was someone I’d known a day, who already considered us friends.

‘If you stay here tonight,’ I suggested, ‘we’ll find you somewhere better to hide tomorrow – what d’you say?’

Anna looked relieved and uncomfortable at the same time.

'Thank you,' she said quietly. 'If there's anything I can do for you . . .'

I held up the jar of antiseptic. 'You already have.'

'And Ray'll be cool with helping?'

'He'll be totally up for it,' I assured her. 'He's bound to know a decent hiding place round here.'

The arsenic part of things would alarm Ray, admittedly: I was worried about that myself, and I was all for going straight to his house to tell him right away. But then Nan's voice boomed across the yard.

'Stevie? What you up to? Bring that dog into the warm before she catches her death!'

Anna froze.

'Hell, is she coming?' She hissed.

I listened. Hearing nothing, I shook my head. Thankfully, Nan had stayed on the doorstep.

'Your nan likes Flea too, huh?' Anna whispered.

'Everyone does. Dogs are much more straightforward than people.'

She kissed the top of Flea's head before passing her back to me. 'Amen to that.'

*

I didn't think I'd sleep that night. What with Anna outside again, and poisoners lurking about, my brain kept whirling. Yet by the time I'd changed into my pyjamas, I felt dead on my feet. But I'd forgotten all the junk that'd fallen off the wardrobe, and still needed tidying away. On the other side of our bedroom barricade, Bev was already in bed.

'Hurry up so I can turn the light out.' She yawned loudly.

There were boxes of old toys, a suitcase, a hat box. Most of it I just shoved under the bed, but the suitcase wouldn't shut properly again. When I opened it to try and fix it, I recognised Dad's old work bag folded up inside. The buckles, the front pockets where he'd keep a pencil, all so familiar. I'd not seen the bag for two years, but the old feeling – the unbearable ache in my throat – was suddenly there again. I sat back on my heels, thrown. Mum had got rid of most of Dad's things. The good stuff went to Uncle John, Mum's brother who lived in Scotland, the not-so-good to the church jumble. She'd hung on to a few special bits – the tie he wore on their first date, his war medals, the hankies she'd often slip into her pocket, his wedding ring. I wondered why she'd kept this particular bag.

When Dad came in from work he'd hang up his work bag in the hallway: it was the best way of telling if he was home. After he died, it stayed hanging there for months. No one had the heart to move it. But in the end, I asked Mum to take it down because it kept tricking me into thinking Dad was back. It made everything sadder, and life was sad enough already.

I lifted the bag out of the suitcase. The buckles were so stiff, they didn't want to open, and when Bev started moaning about switching the light off again, I almost gave up. But there was something in the bag, I could feel it. And when one of the buckles finally gave, I lifted the flap to see inside.

The smell hit me first: coal-tar soap and engine oil. It was still strong enough to make me catch my breath. Then I saw something red and knew it was Dad's favourite jumper, the old one he dug the allotment in, that Mum had to pester him into taking off. I started to pull it out of the bag; as I did so the jumper crackled. There was something papery hidden inside it.

'What are you doing over there?' Bev called from the other side of the wardrobe.

I stopped. 'Nothing.'

'Well, I'm going to sleep now so you'll have to turn off the light.'

'All right.'

I sat motionless, my mind whirring. I waited for her blankets to stop rustling and her breathing to slow. Then, when all was quiet, I unfolded the jumper. As I did so, an envelope fell into my lap. It was addressed to me:

For Stevie, to be opened on her sixteenth birthday

I felt a bit dizzy. Like my heart was going too fast and I needed more air. It was seeing Dad's handwriting again that set me off, because it was as if I was hearing his voice. I stared at the envelope. I wouldn't be sixteen for another five years: I'd burst having to wait that long to read it.

Anna, I'd bet, would open the envelope straight away. She wouldn't wait just because someone told her to. And what if there was a war between America and Russia, and I never got to read Dad's letter at all?

That decided it: little finger under the flap, I opened the envelope as quietly as I could. Inside were three pages of a letter.

'*To Vie . . .*' it said. My throat thickened.

The date in the right-hand corner was 20 June 1960, which, by my quick reckoning, was about three weeks before Dad died. Then came a great block of jagged writing. By squinting at it, I could make out the words 'test' and 'protection', but the rest was a blur on the page.

I'd always struggled with Dad's handwriting. And three pages of it, with my slow reading, felt like an awful lot to get through. I'd half a mind to leave it, and show the letter to Bev in the morning. Or perhaps I should put it back in the suitcase.

'*By the time you read this . . .*' the first line said.

I took a deep breath, and using my finger to follow the words, started to read.

20 June 1960

To Vie,

By the time you read this you'll be a young woman with all your life ahead of you. Had things been different we'd have sat down together, like Bev and I did earlier this year, and had a father–daughter chat about your future. Sadly, as things turned out, that's not to be, so instead, I'm writing down what I need to tell you.

It all began with a secret I was asked to keep, and, out of loyalty, I did keep it, for far too long. But what I've learned, Vie, is that sometimes things happen in life that are too important to keep quiet about. It's then that you have to decide: will you ignore it, hope it goes away, or will you be brave and speak up, even if every last bit of you is terrified and embarrassed and thinks no one will listen? In this letter is an account I've been instructed never to share. But now that time is running out for me I have to tell someone, and that someone is you.

You'll remember the last time I went away to work, when I came home again with a suntan? Well, that was 1958, and the job was on an island in the middle of the Pacific Ocean, where I witnessed the testing of nuclear bombs.

'Go home,' they said afterwards. 'Forget what you saw, and get on with your lives.'

Most of us were soldiers who were – pardon the pun – dying *to live a normal life, after twenty or so years in the army. I was happily married to your mum, with two young daughters (that's you and Bev!), living in a decent house in a nice, quiet area with fields at the back of us. I was itching to get on with civilian life. I'd a mechanic's job at the garage lined up, and an allotment down the road where I had plans to start growing all our own vegetables.*

It was one last trip abroad, they told us. The money would help pay for a new kitchen boiler, and I'd be away for two months. No one told us where we were going, or the reason for the trip. But it was a very long, boring journey: two flights, both over seven hours. Someone said we were flying over Africa at one point, but mostly all I saw from the plane window was sea.

The island where we landed didn't yet have a runway, so the pilot brought us down with a terrific bump on the flattest strip of land he could find. We thought we'd arrived in paradise. I'd never seen such a beautiful place – blue sea, blue sky, palm trees and beaches in every direction, and a heat on my skin that I'd never known in England, not even on a hot summer's day.

What was *slightly odd were the empty buildings scattered along the roadside. The locals had left ahead of us because we were here to do something so top secret no one could know about it – not even us, so it seemed.*

Our camp was in the sand dunes behind the beach. Once the tents were up, we were free for the rest of that day – and the days following – to go swimming, to sunbathe, to lounge about in hammocks. It was as if we'd been sent there for a holiday.

When the work finally started, we were still in good spirits. Our job was to build proper roads, runways so planes could land safely, a control tower, rooms for the senior commanders. No one asked why we were doing it, what all this was for, but the day came when everything was ready, and we were told by an official in a smart white suit that we had nothing to fear.

A few people started to worry then. Why would the man mention fear if everything was going to be fine? Why were they not telling us what we were there to do? Why was it all such a secret? The very next day we discovered the truth.

The only orders we'd been given were to wear long trousers, and to meet on the grass outside the officers' mess at two o'clock. It was a blisteringly hot day. I can still remember the sun burning the back of my neck as we sat in rows, cross-legged like schoolboys. The same man in the white suit addressed us through a megaphone.

You are here to witness the test of a hydrogen bomb, he said. There is no danger to you. Everything has been specially calculated.

He pointed to the sky, where the tiny silver shape of a plane was already circling. The bomb will be dropped from the plane into the sea. All we ask is that you follow our instructions.

We'd heard of these super-weapons the Americans and Soviets were building, bombs a thousand times more powerful than the ones used in the previous war on Japan. It was a thrill, an honour, to be part of such an important project.

The first instruction was for us to turn away from the sea. Then, just forty seconds before the bomb was to be dropped, we were told to shut our eyes and cover them with our hands. I braced myself for a deafening noise.

But it was the light that came first. A flash through the back of my head. I saw every single bone in my hands, lit up like an X-ray. Then came a wave of such intense heat, I thought I was about to catch fire.

Now turn around, the man with the megaphone told us. It was a strict order. We had no choice. Turn and look straight ahead and you'll see the test has been successful.

I turned, opened my eyes. I'll never forget the sight.

Out over the sea, there was no blue sky left. That huge, angry, boiling cloud of greys, greens, reds had swallowed everything, even the sun. It was too hot to breathe. Flames fell from the air; only later I realised it was the birds, catching fire as they flew. Then came a wind, a pressure so strong it knocked us flat to the ground.

I must have lost consciousness because the next thing I felt was water on my face. It was raining. Odd, when there'd been no clouds in the sky. It wasn't normal rain – this was black and smelled briny like the sea. All around me, men were standing up, shaking their heads in disbelief. A few were too stunned to move.

The next day the clean-up began. There were dead birds everywhere, and so many dead fish they were like a skin across the surface of the sea. We were told not to eat them, but a few of the men did. They told us not to go swimming, either. The holiday was over.

There were more bomb tests in the weeks that followed. From then on we had to take cover when, after the initial explosion, the pressure wave hit. And the rain, we soon learned, was seawater sucked into the air by the vacuum the bomb had created, made black by radioactive dust. Though we were reassured our long trousers were fine, more and more of the commanders started wearing full protective clothing.

There was no more fresh fruit: the trees had burned down, the houses were scorched. Black mud got into our water, our clothes, and the smell of rotting fish hung over everything. Our island paradise quickly became hell on earth.

What we were witnessing was the aftermath of nuclear bombing. These were the weapons of the future, so the experts claimed, weapons nobody wanted to use *because they didn't dare to. No world leader would attack another country if they feared nuclear reprisals. Some even called them peaceful bombs. America and the Soviet Union were both building their arsenal, which was why our country had to join in the race.*

On the island, none of us men talked about what we'd seen. We didn't ask questions. We got on with clearing mud and fish, building roads, watching strange mushroom clouds appear in the sky. We were soldiers. Once the tests were over, we shut the door on what we'd seen, and pulled the bolt across.

When the time came to go home it was drummed into us: the tests you have witnessed are 'classified information'. Do not tell your wives, your children, your parents, your friends. Forget what has happened. Get on with your lives.

I came home to you, my family. You were busy at school, already loving dogs more than books. I went to work at the garage, grew potatoes on my allotment.

Life was steady and decent: I had plenty to be grateful for.

Then, two years later, I developed a cough that wouldn't go away. Eventually, when I went to the doctor, the X-rays and blood tests showed something was wrong. Others I knew from the trip were also becoming unwell – skin complaints, sight loss, breathing problems, strange illnesses that no one could put a name to.

Don't talk about what you saw on the island, we'd been told. But we started to, between ourselves, because we knew it was no coincidence. All that mud we swept up, all those fish we handled, everything was polluted with fallout from the test bombs. We'd been healthy young men when we'd gone to the island. We came back with a death sentence hanging around our necks.

The doctors offered us treatments that didn't work, operations that made things worse. My arms turned black and blue from all the blood tests – you might remember that.

I got so tired of hospitals, Vie. All that travelling to and fro. If there had been a magic pill to make me better, I would've taken it. I would have jumped at the chance just to try. But there was nothing to *try.*

Scientists had been too busy making those terrible bombs to find a cure for what was wrong with me.

And it was all a lie. There is no such thing as a peaceful bomb. Once those weapons are in existence, there's always the risk that someone, one day, will be angry or mad enough to use them. If that ever happens, please don't stay silent.

Vie, you're more like me than anyone: you'd rather keep your head down and not make a fuss. So, now you're ready to face the world as a grown-up, let me tell you this: the best weapon of all is your own voice. Don't walk away. Don't be the quiet one who lets other, louder, more powerful people decide how life will be. Listen, yes, but don't ever be afraid to speak.

Yours, always with love,

Dad

Day Three

RUSSIANS DENY DEADLY MISSILES
AIMED AT AMERICA

The Daily Times, Thursday 25
October 1962

8

Ray was still eating his cornflakes when I arrived. He didn't look especially pleased to see me.

'Is Flea okay?' he asked, warily. ''Cos you're a bit early for school.'

All the Johnsons – bar Ray's dad – were there, having breakfast, passing the jam, the butter, the milk, so the whole table was a tangle of stretched arms and sharp elbows. Mrs Johnson pulled out a chair for me. I'd rather have spoken to Ray in private, but reluctantly, I sat down.

'Flea's fine,' I told him, feeling awkward because everyone else seemed to be listening. 'Sorry if I was horrid about it. I didn't mean to be.'

'Phew to that.' Ray smiled, which I took to mean we were pals again.

'And,' I dropped my voice, 'I've got OTHER IMPORTANT NEWS.'

We exchanged meaningful looks, which Mrs Johnson

noticed. 'About time you had that fringe of yours trimmed, Stevie. It's making you rather boss-eyed.'

'Ask your nan to do it,' Pete advised. 'She's staying with you, isn't she?'

'She is,' I muttered, supposing Ray must've told him.

'She looks groovy, your nan,' said Rachel, who was covering her toast with jam and marmalade together.

Groovy wasn't a word I'd use to describe Nan. If she knew what Dad had written to me, I didn't know what she'd make of it. I was still trying to take it in myself. The letter was here with me, folded up, in my skirt pocket, because I wasn't sure what else to do with it.

*

'Well? What's the important news?' Ray demanded, the second we'd left his house – thankfully without Rachel, whose friend was better today. 'You look like you haven't slept a wink.'

I kept quiet until we'd passed number two, where a window cleaner was working outside. The 'To Rent' sign had been taken down, I noticed, and curtains were now hanging inside, as if someone was about to move in.

Once we'd hit the safety of the waste-ground path, I told him.

'Anna's back.'

Ray slowed right down.

'Jeepers! What about the thing she was collecting?'

'*Person*,' I corrected him. 'It went wrong. Says she's going to try and get him again in a few days.'

'Him? So it's a boy? Or a man? Could be a brother or a friend or a cousin—'

'It's the "in a few days" part I'm more concerned about,' I interrupted.

'Because of your nan staying, right?'

'Right. And . . .' I did a quick glance behind me. 'You know Anna's being followed? Well, apparently they're trying to poison her – with arsenic.'

Ray stopped completely. '*Arsenic?* Whoa! I thought I was the one with the big imagination!'

'I don't think she's making this up,' I pointed out.

Ray ran a hand over his head, clearly worried. 'I dunno, Vie. This is starting to sound a bit much.'

'I promised we'd help her, though.'

'Without asking me first?' He rolled his eyes. 'Geez, shouldn't the police be dealing with this?'

'I did try saying that to Anna. She won't have it.'

'But arsenic's serious. It gets your kidneys and your liver, and everything else – plus it makes you stink of garlic,' he said, not able to resist a random fact.

'Look, all we have to do is find her a safer place to hide,' I replied.

We walked on past the first of the building plots. Already the foundations for the second and third houses were being laid. We'd have to find a new shortcut to school soon. Ray, meanwhile, had gone quiet, head down, hands in pockets. I supposed he was getting used to the idea that Anna and her complicated world had come back into ours.

'So,' I said, shifting my school bag to my other shoulder. 'Got any bright ideas for decent hiding places?'

I followed Ray's gaze across the waste ground. We lived in a town, that was the trouble. Everywhere was busy. Even the waste ground was teeming with workmen these days – at least, most of it was.

'D'you think there really is an old pillbox under that lot?' Ray was pointing at the far corner of the furthest field. The building work hadn't reached there yet: it was still a tangle of long grass and brambles.

'Bev reckons so, but I've never seen it.' I realised then what he was getting at. 'D'you think we should check it out, for Anna?'

'Yeah. In daylight would be best.'

'We've got school, though.'

'Aha! Exactly!' Ray wrinkled his nose, which meant he had the beginnings of a plan.

*

Thursday's lessons started with music and movement, which Ray hated because it involved dancing, and I loved because it was like PE. We had to go to the dining hall, where there was space to run about, and an enormous radio set screwed to the wall. The hall was always freezing. It didn't help that we had to strip down to our vests and gym knickers, and wait while our teacher Miss Elliott tried to find the right radio station. Today the radio was being especially temperamental, so we were told to go and stand by the lukewarm radiators. I beckoned Ray to the furthest one, away from the rest of the class.

'Ready to share your plan, brainbox?' I asked, once we were sitting with our backs against the radiator.

'Pigs,' Ray replied. 'It's the one way we can get out of school after lunch without breaking any rules.'

Pig*swill*, was what he actually meant.

Every afternoon, two pupils were chosen to take the kitchen scraps half a mile up the lane to Cuckoo Farm. It was a messy, muddy, awkward job, and the farmer, so people said, would set his dogs loose if he didn't like the look of you. I didn't remind Ray of this fact. More importantly, Cuckoo Farm's land bordered the last waste-ground field, right at the place where the pillbox was meant to be.

'You're a genius, you are,' I told Ray.

'Ah well, if you say so.' He grinned. 'I'll ask Miss Elliott if we can go.'

'You don't ask, you get *picked*,' I reminded him. 'By Dr Elson.' He was our headmaster, and had the pale, withered look of a vampire needing supper. Certainly, I'd never dared speak to him, and didn't think Ray had, either.

I shut up then because Harvey Brooker, the class clown, was coming over. Trailing him were Tanya Hardy and Meena Kumar, two of the popular girls in our class. I guessed it was the radiator they wanted, not our company.

'Shove up, Johnson.'

Harvey Brooker always spoke to Ray like that – rude, pushy: I wondered why Ray put up with it. Still, we both shuffled along to make room, which meant Harvey Brooker now had the warmest part of the radiator.

'What's the point in school when we're about to be blown up?' Tanya was saying. She did ballet: you could tell by the graceful way she sank to the floor, rather than sitting down like a normal person.

Harvey Brooker yawned. 'Won't happen, T. No one'll actually use those bombs. The thought they *might* is enough to put anyone off, that's what my ma told me.'

It was what Nan believed too: Dad didn't. In his view, if nuclear weapons existed, there was always a risk someone, some day, *would* use them.

Tanya's attention turned to Ray. 'Your dad's American. D'you reckon he'll be fighting if this war kicks off?'

'You're talking to me?' Ray was a bit taken aback, because normally Tanya ignored him.

She gave him a withering look. 'You're the only American in our class, aren't you? I suppose you've got family out there too?'

'Yup.' Ray nodded, coolly. 'Aunts and uncles and cousins, all living close enough to Cuba to get hit if they fire their missiles.'

It felt horribly real, hearing him say this. That actual people, who we knew, could be in the firing line.

'It can't happen! It's pointless!' I blurted out. 'They can't be that stupid, these politicians. No one'll win!'

Tanya and Meena stared at me. To be fair, it was

probably the first time I'd ever said a word in front of them. Even Ray looked surprised at my outburst.

I shrugged, a bit embarrassed. 'Just saying, that's all.'

But usually I'd have said nothing, and it made me wonder if some of Anna's confidence was starting to rub off on me.

*

All through our next lesson, I pondered the pigswill errand. How would *we* get picked, when Dr Elson probably didn't even know our names? On the wall behind Miss Elliott's desk was a pinboard full of things students had made for her – cards, dried-out daisy chains, a bad drawing of a dog from me. She was everyone's favourite teacher. Taking the pigswill would be easy – a done deal – if we could simply ask her.

Today's lesson was about autumn. We'd each been given our own dead leaves to study, so our desks were awash with bright oranges, yellows, reds and purples. At the front, Miss Elliott told us to choose one leaf and feel its texture, to smell it, to imagine the tree it came from. I was aware of Ray to my right, his knee jiggling under his desk. Neither of us was concentrating.

'Your leaf comes from a tree that has survived

droughts and storms. Next spring it'll make new leaves, and on goes the cycle,' Miss Elliott was explaining when Harvey Brooker's hand shot up.

'Not if the Russians get us first, miss,' he remarked, smirking like he'd said something clever.

Miss Elliott flinched. 'Perhaps we'd better not—'

'But a tree wouldn't survive a nuclear bomb, would it, miss?' Tanya joined in.

'Nothing would. We'd all be DEAD,' Harvey boomed.

I'd never actually seen the colour drain from someone's face, but that was exactly what happened next to Miss Elliott.

'Excuse me, children,' she said quietly.

We twisted in our seats to watch as she left the room.

'Where's she gone?' Meena asked.

When, after ten minutes, Miss Elliott hadn't returned, Tanya said she'd go to the school office and find out. She came back with Mr Reilly, the drama teacher, who barked at us to put our work away.

'The headmaster wants to have words with you lot,' he said, sounding thoroughly annoyed.

'We're in BIG trouble,' Tanya whispered, as we filed out of the classroom to the main hall.

What concerned me more was the pigswill. This wasn't the way to get Dr Elson's attention. What slim chance we had of being picked at all was rapidly slipping away.

But ours wasn't the only class in trouble. The whole school – three hundred students – had been herded into the main hall. A spreading silence announced the headmaster's arrival. Dr Elson was wearing his black academic gown, and swept up on to the stage like a very large bat.

'I am disappointed,' he addressed us. 'Disappointed that you lack the discipline to keep your emotions in check. You are children, not politicians. Some of you are taking advantage of the situation in Cuba, and getting rather above yourselves.'

Dr Elson scanned the audience, the light catching his spectacles so they glinted like shields. I felt myself swaying as I tried to keep still.

'This morning, a valued member of our school was sent home, too sick with worry to continue her work,' Dr Elson said. 'All because of a silly conversation in class.'

I felt awful. He was talking about Miss Elliott. We hadn't meant to upset our teacher – even Harvey Brooker, with his big mouth, probably wished he could take back his stupid comments. Still, I felt horribly guilty. Our teacher was scared, just like we were, and we'd gone and made her feel worse.

'These are difficult times, I accept.' Dr Elson softened his tone, before coming at us again, bullet-hard. 'But we will *not* discuss the current conflict in lessons. We will *not* second-guess the outcome. And we most certainly will *not* spread hysteria about nuclear warfare! Do I make myself clear?'

A drone of 'Yes, sirs' filled the hall, and we were dismissed early for lunch.

9

'Now what do we do?' I said to Ray, as we gobbled down our spam fritters.

We needed another excuse to get out of lessons. If not, we'd have to wait till after school, after my paper round, to search for an old shelter that might or might not exist. And by then it would be too dark to find it, anyway.

'I'm thinking,' replied Ray, who'd already moved on to his jam roly-poly.

But thinking got us nowhere. By the end of lunch, the whole situation felt hopeless. It was as we stacked our plates at the dining-hall hatch, that Ray gave me a sharp nudge: 'They've not been collected yet, look.'

He meant the buckets into which we scraped our leftovers for the pigs. Already, they were full to the brim, the surrounding floor splattered with custard and trampled peas.

'Look at the mess!' one of the dinner ladies cried, crossly. 'Where the devil are my bucket carriers today?'

Before I'd even fully understood, Ray had pulled me out of the queue and was steering me through the swing doors into the kitchens. The room was fogged with steam. Though there hadn't been any for lunch that day, a depressing smell of cabbage hung over everything.

'We're to take the pigswill, Stevie Fisher and I,' Ray announced to the angry dinner lady.

I prayed his confidence would convince her. But in all honesty, she was more concerned about the state of the serving hatch.

'What kept you both?' she demanded, then flapped her hand. 'Oh, never mind, you're here now. You know the path to Cuckoo Farm, do you?'

'Yes, miss,' Ray replied.

I nodded, leaving the talking part to Ray. It struck me that he hadn't lied, he hadn't pretended we'd been picked by Dr Elson. He'd simply stated the truth: we *were* taking the pigswill, thanks to him.

*

To the right of the school caretaker's cottage was a gate that pupils weren't normally allowed through. Beyond it was a narrow path that led to Cuckoo Farm. The pigswill buckets were heavy, filled with pink spam and yellow custard, and unrecognisable half-chewed mouthfuls of food.

'D'you think pigs *like* spam?' I asked Ray, as we walked. 'I mean, it's pork, isn't it?'

He shrugged. 'Maybe Cuckoo Farm's pigs are cannibals.'

Pausing to rest our arms, we saw the farm up ahead – a red-brick house surrounded by field after field of mud, dotted with little tin-roofed sheds for the pigs. An old man in a filthy tweed jacket came out to meet us. I assumed he must be the farmer. Behind the gate, two huge collie dogs were growling and baring their teeth. Once I'd dropped my bucket over the gate, I left my hand dangling just long enough for the collie dogs to sniff. They approached warily, tails and ears low.

'I wouldn't,' the farmer warned. 'They've been going mad all morning. There's a stray dog on the loose about the place and they don't like it.'

I took my hand away.

'It isn't a big white dog, is it, with a squished-up face?' Ray asked.

The farmer rocked back on his heels, eyeing us both. 'Know who owns it, do you?'

'Nope,' Ray said quickly.

'Well, if you find out, you tell 'em, if I catch that dog on my land again, it'll be a bullet between its ears.'

*

'That's the same dog that bit Flea, isn't it?' I said, once we'd left the farm. '*Do* you know who it belongs to?'

'No,' Ray admitted. 'But it's interesting that it turned up more or less the same time as Anna, don't you think?'

'*Did* it?' I hadn't considered this.

'Maybe I'm overthinking. We don't know she's even got a dog. I mean, we hardly know anything about her, do we?'

'Well, she likes ginger biscuits and going to the cinema. She doesn't enjoy asking for help,' I said, listing what we *did* know. 'She never takes her hat off – there's a few to be getting on with. Oh, and it's a *person* she's collecting, remember. A *him*.'

'And we think she went to the Co-op on Havana Road,' Ray added.

I nodded. 'For ginger biscuits, maybe.'

We walked on briskly. The earlier sunshine had long gone. A cold wind buffeted us, making the bare-twigged hedges on either side of the path chatter like old bones. We didn't have long to find the pillbox: school would be expecting us back within the hour. At the next five-bar gate, I stopped to get our bearings.

'The waste ground starts the other side of that hedge.' I pointed diagonally across a muddy field that had, by the smell of it, recently been home to more pigs.

Beyond the hedge itself was the same daunting mass of brambles and stinging nettles we'd seen earlier from the waste-ground side. We were in the right place, more or less.

Clambering over the gate, we dropped down into the pig field. In school shoes, the mud was slippery, the pig smell so strong it made my eyes water. Ray yanked his jumper up to cover his mouth and nose. The boundary, when we reached it, was a deep, nettle-ridden hedge.

'Bet you there's a way through,' I said, and followed the line of the hedge until I found a gap where a badger or fox had forced its way in.

'I'll go first,' I offered. 'Just to check what's down there.'

The track was so small and narrow I had to crawl along it, stopping every few yards to unhook my hair or coat sleeve from the thorns. Ten yards in, I came face to face with what was, indeed, a wall. I couldn't believe our luck.

‘It’s here!’ I called out to Ray.

Crashing and grunting, Ray heaved himself through the hedge to join me. Moments later, we were on our feet again, standing in what looked like a doorway. A thick net of ivy hung across it.

‘This must be the way in,’ Ray said, reaching up to clear the greenery away.

‘Leave it. It’s camouflaging everything.’

We found another way in through a hole in the wall.

Inside, the shelter was one hexagonal room. The walls were brick, the floor bare earth. It smelled of foxes and mouldy leaves, and was far bigger than I expected.

‘It’s got to be four times the size of our coal shed!’ I cried in delight.

‘Ace, isn’t it?’ Ray agreed.

‘You suggested it,’ I reminded him.

Sure, it needed a bit of a spruce-up. There were beer bottles lying around, cigarette ends, the ashes of a campfire. Someone had written ‘Tommy 4 Eva’ on the wall. Yet from the state of the ivy over the door, I didn’t suppose anyone had been here for a long while. It really was a brilliant hiding place. The brambles and nettles would put most sensible people off. And if, like Anna, the poisoners weren’t local, they’d have no idea the pillbox was here.

‘What can we do to make it cosy?’ I asked, because the litter and the damp smell weren’t exactly welcoming.

‘I can get more blankets, a cushion – oh, and what about a torch?’ Ray offered.

‘Fab. I’ll get food. And a hot-water bottle.’

Between us, we made a list of what to bring up after I’d done my paper round. Now we’d found it once in daylight, it shouldn’t be hard to find again in the dark. I couldn’t wait for Anna to see this place. It was going to be the best secret hideout ever made.

‘Do you think we need curtains?’ Ray said.

I laughed. ‘Isn’t that going a bit far?’

But I’d been so excited, I hadn’t noticed the pillbox had a window. It wasn’t a proper one with glass, but long and narrow like an arrow slit in a castle. Though it was overgrown, some light came through the leaves. Underneath the opening was a ledge, about knee high, made of more bricks.

‘They’d have rested their guns on that,’ Ray said, realising what I was staring at. ‘Or their flasks of tea.’

He meant soldiers in the last war, men like his dad and mine, keeping watch for the enemy. Not poisoners, admittedly, but the situation still felt uncomfortably close to home.

From outside came a low humming sound. It undercut the blackbirds and the thrushes, and the distant traffic roar.

'Can you hear that?' I asked.

Ray nodded. 'Is that the electric fence? It sounds pretty close.'

'Help me up,' I pleaded, because the window itself was too high for me to reach.

Leaning on Ray's shoulder, I got on to the ledge. He climbed up beside me. Through the narrow opening and the ivy, brambles and knotweed, we saw the glinting metal of the airbase fence. It was almost close enough to touch – if you had a death wish.

'Wow!' I breathed.

From this angle, the view into the airbase was amazing. Usually, all we ever saw of it was grass, tarmac, maybe someone checking the weather instruments in the little white box that stood near the runway.

Today, inside the fence, there were twenty or more people walking about. They were all wearing overalls and measuring distances and writing things on clipboards. Someone in a little buggy-type vehicle kept whizzing between them to check what they were doing. In the distance, near the runway's end, the doors stood open on a row of aircraft hangars. We were too far away to see what was inside, but I could guess, and my heart thumped so hard I could feel it in my throat.

American planes to drop American bombs on Russia. And if the Russians fought back, that would make the airbase here in Britain, just a stone's throw from where we lived, a target.

'I wonder if my dad's down there?' Ray whispered. He shifted left, craning his neck until he spotted Mr Johnson. 'There he is! That's him, with the tape measure!'

I had to look twice to be sure. Because this man with the tape measure was shouting. We were too far away to hear the exact words, but from the way he was waving his arms he seemed furious. It took the edge off my excitement, and I turned away from the window.

'I've never seen your dad angry like that,' I remarked.

Ray rubbed his scalp. 'Me neither.'

'No one can win a war like this. It can't happen, can it?'

'It won't, Vie. Kennedy won't want to push the button on a nuclear bomb,' Ray tried to reassure me. 'And if the Russians think he *might* then maybe they'll think twice about what they're doing.'

My hand slipped into my skirt pocket and closed around Dad's letter. The paper crackled like the autumn leaves had done in class.

'Did I ever tell you what my dad did in the last

war?' I said.

'Sure, he was in the army.'

'He was. In France, rescuing people whose houses had been bombed. He always said you'd be amazed at the damage even a small bomb can do. Then, last night, I found this.'

I took out the folded paper and shook it at him slightly. 'Read it, will you?'

*

On the walk back to school Ray grew quieter and quieter. I'd never seen him so lost for words.

'Are you okay?' I asked. ''Cos you don't seem it.'

He gave his usual 'Just thinking' answer, but was shaken up, I could tell. Perhaps showing him Dad's message wasn't such a great idea, after all.

Back in the classroom we sat at our desks, sharpened our pencils, worked through our history lesson like everyone else, though Ray still looked dazed. It scared me, rather. Maybe it would've been better to show the letter to Bev, or put it back in the suitcase, or better yet, not have opened it in the first place.

By the end of the school day, Ray was more talkative, which was a relief, because we still had to sort out Anna and the pillbox. He didn't mention Dad's letter again, so nor did I, not yet. But if Ray's reaction was anything to go by, that letter was dynamite. From now on I'd need to be careful who, if anyone, I told.

10

'A Second World War pillbox? How cool!' Anna was thrilled when I told her later that afternoon. 'You and Ray, you're a pair of legends!'

I'd expected to find her asleep, but she was pacing the tiny space between the coal heap and the back wall. She was all nervous energy today. Eyes, fingers, her long, long legs – none of her could keep still.

'Wait till you see it,' I said eagerly. 'It's ace inside. A proper den!'

At least it would be, when Ray and me had tidied it a bit. My paper round done, we were heading straight up there now, once I'd raided our larder.

'We'll come for you at seven o'clock tonight, okay?' I told her.

'Sure thing, boss!' Anna grinned, did her silly Scout salute, then asked, super-casually, 'What's going on out there in the big wide world today?'

'With Cuba?'

'No, round here. Out in the street.'

'I haven't seen anyone suspicious hanging about, if that's what you mean.'

'Oh. Okay.' Her forehead puckered into what might've been a frown: her eyebrows were so faint it was hard to see them. 'That's good.'

For now, maybe. The poisoners were out there, somewhere. She'd be so much safer in the pillbox.

*

Daylight was fading as I rang Ray's doorbell. I'd brought sandwiches, cake, a flask of tea, candles and matches, and two extra sweaters. It'd been risky, trying to smuggle everything past Nan, and in the end I'd had to scream 'Spider!' from the bathroom to get her to leave the kitchen at all. Now, though, my school bag was bulging. I gave it a satisfied pat.

'Oh!' I said, surprised when Ray came to the door without his shoes on. 'Aren't you ready?'

Behind him on the hall floor was his rucksack, stuffed with what appeared to be a pillow.

'Almost.' He grimaced. 'My dad's come home and my parents are having—' An argument, by the sound of the shouting coming from the kitchen.

'All of us? Be realistic, Eddie!' Mrs Johnson cried.

'If I can keep it a secret, then the rest of you sure as hell can!' Mr Johnson still sounded cross. 'It's an option, that's what I'm saying. Every airbase family has been offered a place. There's space for all of us.'

Ray and I shared an anxious look.

'Space *where*?' I asked.

'Dunno. I was just listening.'

Beckoning me inside, we crept up to the kitchen door, which was slightly ajar. Mr Johnson was visible through the gap. He was still wearing his work overalls: as a rule, they weren't normally allowed inside the house. Mrs Johnson, though out of view, could be heard clanking cups and slamming drawers.

'Pete won't come, I'll tell you that for nothing,' Mrs Johnson said. 'Not now he's got this new girlfriend.'

Girlfriend? I mouthed to Ray, who seemed as surprised as I was.

'If things get real bad, he might change his mind.' Mr Johnson sighed heavily, head in hands. 'I reckon we're pretty lucky to have somewhere safe to go.'

I didn't notice Ray reach over me to push the door open. The gap we were peering through suddenly widened. Mr Johnson looked round in alarm.

'Stevie! Ray! You scared the life out of me!' he

cried, clutching his chest. 'Not listening at the door, were you?'

We'd been caught red-handed.

'Sorry,' I muttered. 'We weren't ... we didn't mean to ...'

'What's going on?' Ray cut across me. 'What're you fighting about?'

'We're not—' his mum started to say.

Mr Johnson interrupted. 'Why don't you and Stevie go and watch some TV?'

I was all for getting out of there completely, but Ray didn't budge from the doorway.

'What's this safe place you're talking about?' he demanded.

Mrs Johnson, arms folded, leaned against the worktop. She was keeping quiet – deliberately, I reckoned – so Mr Johnson had to answer, which he did after an awkwardly long pause.

'If the Russians attack, we'll be safe, I promise you,' Mr Johnson assured him. 'That's all you need to know.'

'How can anywhere be safe if there's a nuclear war?' Ray argued.

I winced. He was thinking of my dad's letter, wasn't he? Picturing all the dead fish in the sea, the black poisonous mud, burning birds falling from the sky.

Again, Mr Johnson tried to reassure him. 'It won't come to that, son. President Kennedy will make sure of it.'

'Oh, pull the other one, Eddie!' Now Mrs Johnson spoke up – and sharply too. 'You've heard what your sister's been saying. That man promised so much for the people of his country, and what has he *actually* done? Isn't it time you stopped believing everything he says?'

I almost felt sorry for Mr Johnson. Mrs Johnson, my best friend's mum, wearer of spectacles and bobbly cardigans, was quite a force when she put her mind to it.

'I'll tell you what's going on here, Ray. What the big secret is,' Mrs Johnson continued. She seemed to have forgotten I was there too. 'There's a nuclear bunker under the airbase, all right? Your father thinks we can go there and wait things out.'

'It's incredible down there,' Mr Johnson tried to convince him. 'Everything's radiation-proofed so we'll be totally safe.'

And I could see Ray wanted to believe him. But then Mr Johnson said, 'We'll have our own bunk beds, food for three months or more.'

Ray stiffened. 'Three *months*?'

'It'll be like going on school camp, or a long boat trip

across the ocean. It'll be a blast!' Mr Johnson promised, reading the look on Ray's face.

'Oh, for heaven's sake!' Mrs Johnson threw up her arms. 'Stop making it sound like a holiday!'

It didn't sound remotely like one to me.

'And after three months, when we come out of the shelter again?' Ray asked. 'Won't we get sick from the radiation?'

Queasiness grew in my stomach. There were no winners in this dreadful situation. The bunker under the airbase, bad as it sounded, was only for the people who worked there. As for the rest of us, in our own homes, we wouldn't even survive three months.

'Listen, son, it's just a precaution,' Mr Johnson tried again. Tried to smile. 'And even if there is an exchange of fire, we've got to believe it won't be that bad.'

An exchange of fire.

'You mean dropping nuclear bombs?' I hadn't meant to say it out loud, but suddenly everyone was looking at me.

'Stevie!' Mrs Johnson's hand flew to her mouth. 'You weren't meant to hear—'

The back door opened before she could finish, and Rachel stomped in with a face like thunder. She threw her school bag down on the table.

'Guess what? There's one measly part in the whole play with no lines whatsoever. And who do they give it to?' She jabbed a finger at her chest. 'Me.'

Just like that, the conversation switched from nuclear bunkers to school plays. Mr Johnson put his arm round Rachel's shoulders, telling her to never give up her dreams.

'You'll have better luck next time, baby,' Mr Johnson said.

'Huh! There won't be a next time,' Rachel huffed. 'I've told Mr Reilly I don't want his stingy part. My acting career is over.'

Mr Johnson's mouth tightened, his mood souring again. 'Who is this *Mr Reilly*? Maybe I'd like to hear him explain why he didn't pick you.'

'Let's go,' Ray muttered to me.

I was glad to.

But out in the hallway, Ray stopped, swaying a little on his feet.

'What if there is a nuclear war, Vie?' he said in a strange, quiet voice. 'What can we do?'

He'd gone very pale, as if he'd just seen a ghost. It scared me.

'I can't do stuff for Anna right now.' He pressed his hands to his face. 'I'm sorry. I – I can't think straight.'

'Yes,' I told him, trying to lower his hands. 'You can.'

Helping Anna right now was the very best thing we could do. It beat sitting around feeling petrified.

Ray shrugged me off. He sank down on to the bottom step of the stairs, knocking over the pile of today's post as he did so. Most of the envelopes slithered to the floor, but the top one landed plum in his lap. It was a blue airmail envelope. The name – 'MASTER RAYMOND JOHNSON' – and address were in huge block capitals. I guessed it was from his cousin Violet in America, who was always writing to him. She told him about life in Alabama, where she lived, and gave Rachel advice on how to do her hair.

When he realised who'd sent the letter, Ray's whole face changed. It was as if someone had flicked a switch and the light came back on. He stood up.

'They're not all ours,' he explained, gathering up the other envelopes. 'It's the postie – he keeps delivering here for number two by mistake.'

'Leave the letters for now,' I begged.

Ray put all the envelopes back in their pile apart from Violet's, which he stuffed in his pocket. He pushed his shoes on, grabbed his coat, then shouldered the big rucksack.

'Okay.' He breathed deeply. 'I'm ready.'

If ever I met Violet, I'd thank her. Because something about her letter made Ray realise he shouldn't – couldn't – give up.

11

The rain falling in a set-in-for-the-evening way, was good news because it meant the waste ground was deserted. Inside the pillbox, I gathered sticks for a fire. Ray cleared away the beer cans and crisp packets. Even without any tidying, I couldn't help think I'd rather be hiding here than in an airbase bunker.

'Be a good spot for sleeping, this,' Ray said, who'd noticed a natural dip in the floor. 'Bit hard and stony, though.'

Once we'd filled it with the dead leaves that had blown inside the pillbox, it was loads better.

On top of the leaves, Ray laid the pillow and sleeping bag he'd brought from home. 'What d'you think?' he asked. 'A passable bed?'

'Try it out.'

Gingerly, Ray lay down. It was almost funny,

watching him sink into the leaves. But he declared it was comfortable and not at all prickly.

'Anna's been sleeping on a coal heap,' I reminded him. 'So it'll probably feel like feathers to her.'

There wasn't much we could do about the damp, mouldy smell. But when we'd finished, the pillbox was looking much more like a cosy den. As well as the leaf bed, we'd made space for a campfire. A night's worth of wood was stacked up, ready. I'd put candles along the brick ledge, unpacked the food and clothes. Ray's contribution of a *Biggles* book and half a chocolate bar completed the haul.

'Looks pretty nifty, huh?' Ray said.

I bumped his shoulder to say it did.

*

Back at ours, Bev had made a cottage pie the size of a football pitch.

'Stay for tea if you like,' I said to Ray.

Though he nipped home to ask his mum, he was back again five minutes later with news that a removal van was being unloaded at number two. Nan was on her feet in a flash, lifting the net curtains.

'I can see a washing machine going in, oh, and that's

a nice sheepskin rug,' she exclaimed. 'Wouldn't have gone with cream leather myself, but I suppose it's all the rage.'

'Are we eating this cottage pie or not?' Bev demanded.

Once we'd had our tea, I began to get properly nervous. Fidgeting, I tried – and failed – to catch Ray's eye. Bev had started yawning. Nan, settling into her chair, moved swiftly on to one of her other favourite topics: why we didn't use our sitting room.

'There's two perfectly decent armchairs in that parlour,' she moaned. 'And a settee and a coal fire, but oh no, we're fine out here in the servants' quarters, aren't we, girls?'

'It's Mum's house, Mum's rules,' Bev replied.

Then, just before seven o'clock, Ray suggested a game of Monopoly.

'Not *now*!' I hissed.

But he'd remembered Bev's competitive streak from when they'd played before. He'd got the measure of Nan too. Within minutes my sister and Nan were arguing over a Community Chest card. And then, a moment later, over the rent on Old Kent Road. They didn't notice Ray putting on his coat, or me clipping on Flea's lead. And when he said goodnight, thanks for tea, and I mentioned I'd walk him home, neither Nan nor Bev looked up from the board.

*

Inside the shed, Anna was on her feet, waiting. She seemed excited. Or maybe it was the cold making her jiggle on the spot, hugging her duffel bag tightly to her chest.

'Am I glad to see you two – sorry, you *three*!' she said, reaching down to scratch behind Flea's ear. 'She's better, isn't she?'

'She's fine,' I assured her. 'Your antiseptic's done the trick.'

'Can we save the dog chat for later, please?' Ray cut in. 'Are we all set?'

Anna nodded.

'Yup,' I said.

'No torches until we get to the pillbox, okay?' he reminded us.

'Loud and clear,' Anna replied.

With Ray leading the way, Anna in the middle and me bringing up the rear, we crept to the bottom of the garden. As Anna's duffel bag swung from her shoulder, I noticed one of the pockets was gaping open. We'd only gone a few steps when something fell out of it – a small book – which I managed to catch.

'Here.' I went to tap her arm. 'You dropped this.'

But I couldn't reach her: she was already crawling through the hedge after Ray. I put the book in my pocket to give back when we got to the pillbox.

Out on the waste-ground path, away from the houses, it hit me just how much colder it'd become. Above us was a sky so clear that even the furthest stars glowed like mist, and from the ground, I could feel the bone-damp chill rising against my legs. Up in front, Ray kept stopping, turning his head to listen. Anna, ever the fidget, bounced on the balls of her feet like she'd springs in her shoes.

'Watch where you're going,' Ray warned, as we picked our way through the building site. Either side of the path were the dark shapes of ditches and wheelbarrows, bricks piled up, ready to be used in the morning.

Clear of this part of the waste ground, we were able to walk faster. When the airbase fence came into view, I felt a stir of real excitement. I couldn't wait for Anna to see inside the pillbox – the leaf bed, the campfire. Hopefully, there'd be time to get a nice, warm blaze going before we had to rush back home.

None of us heard the woman approach.

'Cyril?' The voice came out of nowhere. It made us stop so sharply, we tumbled against each other.

'Cyril? Where are you?'

The woman was heading in our direction. Though she'd not yet seen us, I could make out the silhouette of her coat, her headscarf, an outstretched arm rattling something. There was nothing to hide behind: we were out in the open. Ray waved at us to get down. I crouched, Flea on my knees, praying she wouldn't bark and give us away.

'Crikey, where did she spring from?' Ray whispered.

'Dunno. I don't recognise her, either,' I answered, worried.

Was the stranger following us? Was this one of the poisoners, disguising herself as a dog walker?

My heart was beating double time. Next to me, Anna muttered *blast it* under her breath. The woman passed within ten feet of us. She rattled what seemed to be a tin of biscuits: Flea thought so, anyway, and suddenly wriggled, trying to follow her. I held on as tightly as I could. The woman walked on, still rattling her tin, sounding more and more fed up.

'Cyril? Where are you, you *stupid* creature?'

She'd lost her dog, by the sounds of it, and went on calling him, all the way up to the main road. When she was safely out of sight, I stood up, shaking out my numb legs.

'Phew, that was a bit of a scare!' I smiled weakly.

'Only a dog walker, thank heck,' Ray agreed, scrambling to his feet.

Anna stayed down.

'I've changed my mind,' she said. 'I'm going back to the shed.'

I stared at her. 'You're *what*?'

'But you can't!' Ray insisted. 'It's not safe!'

'Listen.' Anna sighed as if, suddenly, she was very tired. 'They're going to find me. It's only a matter of time. I've got to face them, sooner or later.'

'Someone's trying to poison you, and you're going to give up? I can't believe this!' I cried.

Ray was shaking his head. 'This isn't like you, Anna. What about that *being in charge of your destiny* thing you said?'

'I *am* in charge of what happens to me,' Anna insisted. '*I* decide when I've had enough.'

'Well, you might've mentioned it earlier,' I snapped, thinking of all the effort we'd gone to with the pillbox.

Ray tried a different tack. 'Just come and see your new hiding place, and then decide. It's pretty ace, actually, I think you'll like it.'

I blew my fringe out of my eyes with a furious huff.

'Don't be cross, Stevie,' Anna pleaded. 'This situation I'm in . . . it's . . . it's complicated.'

'Everything's *complicated*!' I cried, before I could stop myself. 'You, me, Ray, this stupid missile business in Cuba. You're not the only one finding life tough. In case you hadn't noticed, the whole world might be about to end!'

There was an ugly silence.

'Geez, Vie,' Ray said, rubbing his head. 'That was a bit sharp.'

I winced. Ray was right: I shouldn't have said it. But the thing was, I was scared too. Reading Dad's letter had left me feeling like I was carrying a terrible weight. Don't keep important secrets too long, he'd said, and I was beginning to understand what he meant. Some secrets were so big they risked overwhelming you.

'I'm sorry, Anna,' I mumbled. 'I don't . . . I'm . . . sorry.'

I half expected her to walk off anyway. But she listened, nodded. 'S'all right, Stevie. I sometimes forget that other people's lives are difficult too.'

'That poor dog walker wasn't having a great night, either,' Ray remarked, trying to lighten things.

But a thought hit me: the dog walker didn't actually *have* a dog with her. She'd lost one called Cyril and was out here in the dark, searching for him. Up at Cuckoo

Farm, Ray had suggested a link between Anna and the dog that bit Flea.

I didn't know what to think. But it made me nervous.

'We'd better get out of here,' I decided.

'Lead the way, captain.' Anna stuck out her hand, and I pulled her to her feet.

*

'Wow! It's incredible!' Anna gasped as soon as she saw inside the pillbox. 'That bed! A real pillow! Oh, and more sweaters, and something to eat. It's totally and utterly *insane*!'

I had to admit our handiwork did look impressive. Once we'd lit the candles and got the campfire crackling nicely, it felt cosier than ever. And safe too, like being in a burrow.

'The outside's covered in brambles. We had a job to find it – and we live round here – so hopefully it'll keep you well hidden,' Ray explained.

'It's so quiet,' Anna observed.

And for a moment, it was. Just the firewood hissing, the electric fence humming outside. Then, also outside, a new noise, low and grumbling, like a truck or a tractor.

Anna cocked her head. 'What's *that*?'

The noise changed in pitch, getting higher and louder. It was coming from the other side of the chain-link fence. Ray went to the little window, pulling aside the undergrowth to see what was happening. Something out there made him stop, mid pull.

'What is it?' I asked, noticing how hard his other hand was gripping the windowsill. 'What's going on?'

He didn't turn around.

'Oh, Vie. It's all kicking off at the airbase.'

12

Too short to reach the window, I hopped up and down on the spot.

'Let me see!' I begged.

Grabbing my anorak hood, Ray yanked me up so my feet found the brick ledge to stand on. The rumbling sound was so loud, I felt the vibrations of it through the wall. Anna squeezed herself in between us.

'Can't see with this lot in the way,' she protested, and tore at the rest of the ivy blocking the window.

Light exploded in our faces. Unable to see anything now, I panicked.

Someone was out there with a torch. Any moment a voice was going to yell at us.

It was the dog-walker woman – no, the farmer.

Men from the airbase, coming to turf us out.

But no one appeared. The rumbling got louder. The light came closer. I was dying to cover my ears but that would mean letting go of the windowsill, and I was desperate to see what was happening.

It was, I realised then, not a person but a vehicle – a truck, a car – coming straight towards us. Dazzling us. Then, like a lighthouse beam, it swung sharply to the left.

We were back in darkness again. As my eyes got used to it, I was able to pick out the long, low shape of an aeroplane.

'Would you LOOK at that!' I cried, though like me, Ray and Anna were mesmerised.

The aeroplane came within touching distance of the fence. The engine-oil smell caught in my throat. I didn't know much about planes, but this one wasn't the big, luxurious kind that flew film stars and presidents around the world. It was small, sharp-nosed. I'd seen similar planes in photographs and on the news in recent days, but never in this old part of the airbase.

As the plane swivelled to face the runway, the white lights became small red ones – tail lights, I guessed. The engine noise reached squealing pitch. A roar, a screech of rubber on concrete, and it rushed away from us. The air rippled with heat. The plane pitched upwards, a bright speck, climbing into the sky.

'That,' Anna said, 'was *incredible*!'

'Wow! Wasn't it?' Ray breathed.

I felt more shocked than excited. Poor Flea, who'd been guarding Anna's ham sandwiches up until now, pawed my foot, whimpering. I stepped down to pick her up and tuck her inside my anorak.

'Sorry, girl,' I whispered. 'That nasty noise is over now.'

But the rumbling started again.

Ray heaved me back up on to the ledge. 'There's more coming! Quick!'

Sure enough, the old runway was adazzle with lights. Plane after plane was queuing up for take-off, making it look like Havana Road at rush hour. The roar and stench of engines made my head spin. The planes kept coming towards us. A flash of white light, then red as they turned. Another blast of noise and heat. Red dots rising up off the ground. On it went, one aircraft after the other: I counted twelve in all.

It was over quick enough. The last plane gone, Flea wriggled to get back to the ham sandwiches. I put her down on the floor, aware I was shaking more than she was.

'V bombers,' Ray confirmed, because he knew stuff like aircraft names.

'Are they going to Cuba?' I asked.

'Soviet Russia, more likely. They're probably just training tonight.'

'Because there isn't a war, *yet*,' Anna reminded me.

'Depends which one you mean,' Ray answered. 'The Cold War's been going on for years. American planes fly along the Soviet border every single day, just in case, well . . . in case they're needed.'

I was horrified. 'What, with nuclear bombs on board?'

Ray nodded guiltily: he'd probably heard it from his dad and knew he shouldn't really be telling us. And part of me wished he hadn't, because my mind filled with images of towns being wiped out, whole cities on fire, until there was nothing left to fight over.

I turned to the window again. No wonder they'd built the pillbox here: the view was incredible. To the right the dark waste ground, and beyond the orange streetlight-glow of World's End Close. But my eyes were drawn back to the airbase. The huge aircraft hangars with their doors wide open. The airbase building where people were working late, the office windows little squares of light. And underneath, deep in the ground, the nuclear bunker Ray's family had been arguing about. There was nothing to see of it, not from up here. But I could picture the bunk beds jammed together, extra-thick doors that closed with special radiation-proof seals. It'd be like living on a submarine or a space ship.

Shivering, I got down from the window to warm my hands at our little campfire.

'Do you think someone *will* press the nuclear button?' Anna asked.

Ray shrugged. 'I don't know.'

'Imagine what it would be like, actually being in a nuclear blast,' Anna mused.

'I'd rather not,' I replied.

Yet, after reading Dad's letter, I *could* imagine it far too clearly: the X-ray flash, the terrible heat like my insides were cooking.

Compared to what was going on in my head, though, Anna seemed amazingly calm. She'd unwrapped the packet of sandwiches and was removing the cucumber, slice by slice, and placing it on the ledge beside her.

'Sorry, I don't like it,' she explained.

But it wasn't the cucumber I was gazing at: it was how relaxed she was. She'd been more terrified by the dog walker than the prospect of a nuclear war.

'Aren't you scared?' I asked, genuinely interested.

Anna swallowed her mouthful of sandwich. 'Yeah, I'm scared of lots of things. But this is different, isn't it?'

'*How?*' Ray and me both said together.

'Well,' she said, wiping butter from her chin. 'You can't run away from a nuclear war, can you?'

'My parents think you can – by hiding in a nuclear bunker for three months,' Ray replied glumly.

'And then what?' Anna insisted. 'All the water will be poisoned, nothing will grow . . .'

'. . . everyone will get sick from the radiation,' I said.

Anna nodded. 'So what's the point?'

'In trying to survive?' Ray looked confused.

'In worrying about what may or may not happen,' Anna answered. 'You're better off trying to change the stuff you can control.'

'Well you could protest against nuclear weapons, for starters,' I said, thinking of Bev.

'True,' Anna agreed. 'It's definitely a way of feeling like you're doing something.'

'What would *you* do, then?' I asked.

She reached for another sandwich. 'I'd try to not be scared, that's what I'd do.'

'You can *do* that?' I wasn't convinced.

But her expression grew eager.

'Imagine if there is a war, and tomorrow is our last day on earth,' she said. 'Would you want to waste it, sitting around being terrified?'

'We'd be in school,' Ray pointed out. 'Which would take our minds off things.'

'Would it?' I said, because we had grammar and

punctuation lessons on Fridays. 'I'd rather be doing something else, frankly.'

'Exactly!' Anna slapped her hands on her thighs. 'Like what?'

'Something really fun. Something I'd never do in a million years,' I decided, warming to the idea. 'Like spend the day with hundreds of dogs.'

'Nice choice. I knew I liked you, Stevie.' Anna grinned. Then to Ray, 'What about you? What's the one thing you dream of doing that would make you completely, utterly, stupidly happy?'

Ray didn't have to think. 'I'd go in a jet plane to America. And meet my cousin Violet in real life, and eat big, thick pancakes in a diner. And see Dr King speaking to a crowd and . . .'

'. . . visit the Statue of Liberty,' I joined in. 'Drive a Cadillac, eat hamburgers.'

'We could, couldn't we? Not go to America, obviously, but we could do something like it tomorrow. Make our wishes come true?' Anna urged.

She was deadly serious, I realised, and my heart gave a funny little hitch. Perhaps there were things we could do together to stop us sitting around, worrying.

Then I remembered.

'Ah, but we're hiding you.'

'And,' Ray added, 'aren't you meant to be fetching—'

'– not tomorrow.' Anna interrupted then went straight back to her idea. 'I could wear a disguise, couldn't I?'

'I bet Nan's got a wig somewhere,' I agreed quickly. 'Or some sunglasses . . . or I could sneak out something of Mum's.'

'What about schoo—' One look at our faces, and Ray stopped himself. 'All right, count me in.'

'What about you?' I asked Anna. 'You haven't said what you'd wish for if it was your last day on earth.'

'I'd go to the seaside, and – if I'm allowed two wishes – have a long hot soak in a bath.'

Ray wrinkled his nose, considering it.

'Yup,' he decided. 'I reckon we can manage both of those.'

*

We agreed to meet at the pillbox at just after eight tomorrow morning. And then – somehow – the three of us would catch a bus out of town to the seaside. It was such a crazy, unlikely idea that I almost believed it could work.

By the time we left for home, it was late. After the cosiness of the pillbox fire, the night felt colder than ever, the grass crunching frostily as we walked. I zipped up my coat, stuffed my hands in my pockets for warmth. It was then I realised I still had Anna's notebook.

I almost asked Ray if we could turn back to give it to her. But, in the distance, the chimes of the town hall clock rang out nine o'clock. We'd been gone two whole hours. I doubted Nan and Bev had the patience to still be playing Monopoly. They'd be wondering where the heck I was.

Back in World's End Close, we stopped briefly outside my front gate.

'Get a good kip tonight, won't you?' Ray said.

I smiled. Sometimes he was like the big brother I never had.

'My brain's still going at galloping pace,' I admitted.

'Mine too. I blame Anna for that.'

I knew what he meant. In the few days we'd known her, we'd done stuff for Anna – with Anna – I never dreamed I'd do. Maybe I wasn't quite as shy and dull as the girls at school made me feel. Thinking this made me feel better about Dad's letter, somehow, as if what he'd said was having an effect on me too.

My hand went to Anna's notebook again. Curious, I took it out and held it under the streetlight. It was about the size of a Christmas card, black, with a hard cover.

'She dropped this earlier,' I explained. 'I forgot to give it back.'

'Go on, open it,' Ray said.

I did, warily. 'The World According to Anna' the opening page declared. I smiled: it was typical Anna. The following page had a date, October 1st, then underneath in scruffy writing – 'Can't write today!' The first few pages looked like shopping lists but with dates from a few weeks ago. The middle part was full of scrawly writing that might've been poems.

'The rest of it is blank,' I said, flicking through to the end of the notebook.

Inside the back cover was a list of three names:

HAVANA ROAD

The first one wasn't a surprise – Anna herself had asked where it was. But what was written underneath made me catch my breath.

FISHER
WORLD'S END CLOSE

I held the notebook at arm's length. 'How does she know my surname?'

'I introduced us both on that first night.' Ray pointed out. 'Though she wouldn't tell us her full name, would she?'

'*That's all you need to know – just Anna*,' I murmured, remembering.

Ray's eyes fell on the notebook again.

'Mind if I have a quick look?' he asked.

I gave the notebook to him, and he riffled through, comparing the final page with the others.

'Gee whiz! It's in the same pen as those first pages!' He showed me the handwriting in blue ink. 'A proper fountain pen too, by the looks of it.'

I didn't see what he was getting at. 'So Anna's only got one pen? What's the big deal in that?'

Ray fixed me with a 'don't be stupid' glare.

'Think about it, Vie. If you were running away, you wouldn't bring a posh fountain pen and ink, would you? I'm guessing she wrote this *before* she left home.'

'But that's crazy!' I whispered.

Because it meant Anna knew my surname was Fisher, she knew I lived at World's End Close, and she knew all of this before she'd even met me.

Day Four

MISSION DESPERATION: PEACE ATTEMPTS FAIL

The Daily Times, Friday 26 October 1962

13

That night, though my sister would've never believed it possible, Bev was snoring loud enough to disturb the whole street. I couldn't sleep at all, though mostly it was my own brain keeping me awake, going over and over what I'd read in Anna's notebook. We'd always known she had secrets, and clever ways of not answering the questions we tried to ask. But this new discovery really unsettled me. If Ray's idea about the pen was right, and Anna knew of me before we'd met, then I needed to find out how and why.

'I'm going to ask her, straight out, tomorrow morning,' I'd decided, before Ray had finally gone home. Then I saw his expression. 'What? I need to know!'

'Yup, you do. *We* do,' he agreed. 'Choose your moment, that's all.'

I wasn't convinced. 'My dad's letter said I shouldn't always keep quiet about stuff.'

Ray sighed. 'I'm just saying, Vie, don't blurt out

something you'll regret. There's probably a simple explanation for it. If that nuclear button gets pressed, none of it will matter, anyway. So try, can't you, to make the most of our day out tomorrow, and ask her when we get back.'

Which was what, in the end, I agreed reluctantly to do. We were off to the seaside for a brilliant day out, and I didn't want to ruin it. Confronting Anna would have to wait. And, as Ray said, there might well be some straightforward, harmless reason for her knowing who I was. In the meantime, we had a day at the beach to enjoy, and despite everything, I was pretty excited about it. I hadn't been to the seaside since Dad died: it was thanks to Anna we were going at all.

We'd decided on Devon, where Ray's family had their holidays. Over the years, I'd heard a lot about Budmouth Point. It was a small town with a lighthouse and a beach, and last summer a little cinema had opened there, which Anna insisted we should go to. It all sounded pretty nice.

According to the timetable there was one direct bus at 9.30 a.m. It was a two-hour journey to Budmouth Point, at a cost of ten shillings each. My paper round money and Ray's piggy-bank savings should be enough to cover our fares. When I'd mentioned that the Budmouth Point locals might recognise Ray and tell his mum he'd skipped school, he'd shrugged it off in a way that was most unlike him.

'I'll think about that afterwards,' he said.

He was right. We were going on this trip to have fun and forget our troubles. We shouldn't waste it worrying about what might happen when we got home.

*

When morning finally came, I dressed as usual in my school skirt and blouse, ponytailed my hair. I wasn't tired in the slightest. If anything, the thrill of where we were going made me buzz with energy.

In the kitchen, the table was covered in paper and paintbrushes. Today was the day of Bev's peace protest at her school, the only obvious sign of breakfast being the toast clamped between my sister's teeth. She was putting the final touches to a banner which said 'SAY NO TO W—'. There were others on the table: 'HANDS OFF CUBA' and 'THE NEXT WAR WILL BE OUR LAST'.

'D'you reckon you'll get in trouble?' I asked, thinking about Dr Elson's harsh warning at our school.

Bev removed the now soggy piece of toast. 'I don't s'pose the teachers will like it much.'

'Don't know what your father would've made of this *protesting* lark, either,' Nan muttered, though she was helping Bev by stacking the signs against the wall once the paint was dry to the touch.

I wished I'd had a chance to show Bev Dad's letter. Despite what Nan said, I *knew* what Dad would've thought of my sister's protest, and it made me feel warm inside, and strong. He'd have said she was using her voice to stand up for what she believed in. I was pretty sure he'd agree with Anna's way of tackling life too – that sometimes you had to seize the moment, which was exactly what we were doing today.

Quickly, I made myself some toast.

'You don't think we've got mice in the larder, do you?' Nan said, suddenly.

I stopped mid bite. 'Mmmm?'

'Well, something's been at the fruit cake and there's four slices of ham missing, and half the bread's gone.'

My toast seemed to take ages to swallow, especially now Nan was watching me like a buzzard.

'Know anything about it, Stevie?' she asked, suspiciously.

All week, I'd expected this moment. We'd been lucky

to get away with smuggling food out for so long. But, though I tried to seem normal, I knew I was acting as guilty as anything.

'Nope, sorry. I'd better go.' Whistling to Flea, I rushed out of the house.

*

When I arrived at the paper shop, Mrs Talbot was still getting my delivery ready. She had a system where she wrote the customer's surname in the top right-hand corner of each paper, her pen currently hovering over a *Daily Express*.

'We've got a new customer in your street. Number two. Burgess is the name,' she announced.

Her eyebrows seemed to think this was interesting news, but I was busy working myself up to ask an awkward question.

'Mrs Talbot.' I took a deep breath. 'Is there any chance you might pay me now, please, rather than later?'

'It's not like you, Stephanie, to be so bold as to ask.'

But when I'd checked my purse on the way here I'd only found four shillings left from last week's wages. I didn't think Ray's savings alone would stretch to three bus fares.

'Please, Mrs Talbot.'

'You know I don't pay anyone early.'

'But what if the world ends?' I begged.

She gave me a narrow look. 'The answer's still no.'

*

Hoping Ray's savings would be enough, I didn't let Mrs Talbot's meanness dampen my mood. And to make doubly sure of it, I didn't read the newspaper headlines or think about Anna's notebook, instead concentrating on what ice creams we'd buy at the seaside – if by some miracle we could afford them. Dad used to get us strawberry ones, sandwiched between two wafers. One time we'd gone to the beach Bev had dropped hers on the pavement, then screamed when all the seagulls swooped down to gobble it up. She'd fought them off like a trooper. I was still smiling remembering it, when I got back to World's End Close.

The one newspaper left in my delivery bag was for our new neighbours at number two, who I now knew were called the Burgesses. Flea followed me up their front path, sniffing all the way. The downstairs curtains were closed, the milk still on the doorstep, but that was hardly unusual given that it wasn't yet half past seven.

As I eased their copy of *The Times* through the letter box, I heard a sobbing noise coming from inside the house. Someone was crying – very hard, by the sound of it. It stirred me up, rather. I stepped back from the door. Today was meant to be a good day – a happy day; I didn't want to think about people being sad. Calling Flea away from a particularly interesting smell, I went home.

*

Back at ours, I packed my school bag with a skirt and blouse of Mum's, Bev's yellow jumper, clean underwear. Most of it, I hoped, would fit Anna.

'Running a bit late today, aren't you?' Nan asked, when she caught me loitering by the kitchen window.

I wasn't: it was only a quarter to eight so, if anything, I was earlier than usual. But Nan's sense that I was up to something was growing.

'Just waiting for Ray,' I answered, though it was his parents I was looking out for. Once they left for work, we'd fetch Anna, and I was eager to get going.

Sure enough, Mr Johnson appeared in his khaki overalls, wheeling his bike out on to the pavement. Then came Mrs Johnson, who worked in town in the library. She walked briskly up the road to where she'd catch the eight o'clock bus. At last, the coast was clear. Yet before I'd even reached our gate, Ray came running across the road.

'You'd better come to mine!' he said, out of breath and in a flap. 'There's a problem!'

Full of dread, I followed Ray back to his house. Yet the problem wasn't Anna, or America or Russia. It was his sister, Rachel, lying on the settee under a blanket. To be honest, I was pretty relieved.

'She's not really ill,' Ray insisted. 'She's just good at acting it in front of Mum.'

Rachel stuck out her tongue.

'She's still in a strop because she didn't get the part she wanted in the school play,' Ray went on.

'No, I'm not,' Rachel answered, *very* stroppily. 'I just didn't feel like going to lessons today.'

Nor did we, to be fair.

But my attention was now on the sound of splashing coming from upstairs. The slap of legs against water. Someone was singing a pop tune very badly – in the bath.

Confused, I pointed at the ceiling. 'Is she *here*?'

'Yup.' Ray grimaced.

This was all wrong. Anna was supposed to be hiding in the pillbox until we went to fetch her. We'd agreed it last night.

'You'll never guess *what*,' added Rachel, who was now sitting up and looking positively enthralled. 'The tall girl upstairs—'

'Anna,' Ray interrupted.

I glared at him: he'd just told his sister Anna's *name*?

'Anna,' Rachel nodded eagerly, 'was throwing stones at his window IN THE MIDDLE OF THE NIGHT! He had to hide her outside until Mum and Dad went to work!'

This certainly wasn't in the plan. Frantically beckoning Ray into the kitchen, I closed the door and rounded on him. 'What the heck is going on?'

'What could I do?' Ray was bewildered. 'Anna turned up here and—'

'So now she knows where *you* live too?' I interrupted.

He raised his palms. 'I dunno. Weird, though, because she got in over the back fence from our neighbours' garden. She wasn't coming from the waste-ground direction.'

I frowned.

'And,' Ray went on, 'she said she'd heard a gunshot near the shelter and panicked. That's why she turned up.'

'A *gunshot*? Cripes!' I let out a long breath. 'D'you think it was them? The poisoners?'

'Could be. Or the pig farmer. Remember what he said he'd do if he saw that white dog again?'

I winced. 'Shoot it. And remember what *you* said, about the dog turning up here around the same time as Anna?'

'D'you think I might be on to something now?'

'Maybe. That woman last night, shaking the biscuit tin? She was out looking for a dog, wasn't she? It could've been the white one.'

'I thought that too.'

'Plus, that's when Anna got scared and wanted to go back to my shed,' I reminded him. 'The dog-biscuit woman frightened her.'

Ray rubbed his head, thinking. 'So there's a link between the dog and the poisoners, is that what we're saying?'

'Maybe. How much does your sister know about all this?' I asked, returning to the problem in hand.

'All I've told her is we've got a new pal who we're helping, and if she tells anyone else, you'll never speak to her again.'

It wasn't much of a threat, but I didn't argue. We'd have to deal with it later, along with everything else.

'Are we going to the beach, then, or what?' I asked.

Ray did one of his cheeky, upside-down smiles.

'I'll say we are!'

I grinned. 'Thank goodness for that!'

*

Since our bus was leaving at half past nine, and if we missed it there wasn't another one, I went upstairs to hurry Anna. Already the plans we'd made in a rush of excitement last night had got complicated, and we hadn't even left the house yet. Still, I was determined to have a great day.

'Anna? I've brought you some clean clothes. I'll leave them out on the landing,' I called through the bathroom door.

The door opened a crack. An arm slipped through, fingers waggling for the clothes, which I handed over. The door closed. Moments later, it opened in a swirl of steam.

'Yes, I know, it's a shock,' Anna muttered, gesturing at her head.

It was hard to see what she meant at first. But as the steam cleared, I realised she wasn't wearing her bobble hat, and this was the first time I'd seen her without it.

'Oh!' I gasped. Her hair was very short – easily as short as Ray's, and he got his clippered by his mum every fortnight. It almost made her look ill, like her eyes were too big for her face. No wonder she wore the hat all the time: it was the sort of bad haircut people would be bound to notice. Or maybe, I suddenly thought, she'd done it on purpose, to disguise herself for our day out at the beach.

'Have you only just cut it off?' I asked, peering around her, expecting to see chunks of hair still lying in the sink.

'What? No!' Anna jammed her hat back on her head, and I got the distinct feeling she didn't want to talk about it anymore.

Sure enough, she went straight into goofy mode.

'What do you think?' she said, posing gawkily like a model.

She was wearing my shirt from home and Bev's yellow jumper: both were too short in the arms. But with her own bright purple cords, she at least looked almost clean, and judging by the glint in her eye, she was ready for some fun.

'Oh, I almost forgot these.' I handed her a pair of old sunglasses I'd found in the kitchen drawer. They might've once been Mum's, or Bev's.

Anna put them on.

'How do I look?' she asked, pouting ridiculously.

'Umm . . . Not like you,' I admitted.

'I look like a film star, don't I? Go on, tell me which one.'

'I dunno . . . Marilyn Monroe?'

Anna pouted even more and wriggled her hips. She looked so funny I burst out laughing. That set Anna off too. The noise of us giggling brought Ray halfway up the stairs.

'You two, honestly,' he remarked, as we tried to get a grip on ourselves. But sharing a laugh had cleared the air: whatever Anna was still keeping from us, she was, most of all, our friend.

Back downstairs in the hallway, Rachel buttoned up her coat.

'I don't know where you're going, but I'm coming with you,' she announced.

'No, you're not – you're ill, remember?' Ray told her.

'Oh, let her come,' I said, partly to hurry things up. I felt sorry for her about the play too, and couldn't see the harm in it now she knew about Anna. 'Though you absolutely mustn't tell a soul, Rachel, okay?'

Rachel nodded solemnly.

'But I've only got eight shillings,' Ray confessed.

'And I didn't get paid early, either,' I admitted. 'So we've not got enough for four bus tickets.'

Ray groaned.

'Hang on. I've got some dosh.' Anna started rummaging in her trouser pocket. With a dramatic flourish, she pulled out a bank note. 'Ta-dahhhhh!'

It was a whole five pounds.

'Wow! That's … um … quite a lot of money,' I stuttered. Five pounds was more than enough for all our bus fares, chips at the seaside, candyfloss, or whatever else we fancied doing at Budmouth Point.

Anna pushed the note into my hands. 'You've done so much for me. I'd feel better if you'd take it. Please?'

As I dithered, Ray quickly accepted. 'That's brilliant of you, Anna, thanks very much.'

'Where did you get—?' I went to say but stopped.

No questions.

Trouble was, there were so many questions building up now – the white dog, the names in her notebook, where the money came from, where *she* came from and why she'd ended up here, in my coal shed and in our lives – but it was already ten past nine.

14

We ran all the way into town, along Havana Road, past the Co-op, the telephone box, the swimming baths where the smell of chlorine wafted out into the street.

'No looking at the news!' I warned, as we zipped past Mr Talbot's newsagent's.

'Or listening,' Ray added, because a couple of old men at the bus stop were discussing the Cuba situation in very loud voices.

'La-la-la!' Rachel covered her ears, singing.

Anna laughed at her. 'Someone's feeling better!'

We all were. Being together, on a seaside mission, was already cheering us up. Yet I also tried to keep my wits about me. Town was busy, even this early in the morning, and I'd not forgotten the poisoners. Any one of these shoppers or people hurrying to work might be following us. And we'd be pretty easy to spot: two mixed-race kids, a tall girl in a bobble hat and sunglasses, and me, the short one, with the fringe in her eyes.

As we slowed to cross the road in front of the bus station, Anna, more out of breath than any of us, put her hand on my my arm.

'Just remember . . .' she puffed. 'No thinking . . . about the war, or school ... or what happens tomorrow, all right? Today is about being here ... in the moment. That's the only rule. Got it, everyone?'

'Got it,' Rachel replied.

'Yup,' I agreed.

'Too right.' Ray grinned.

'Same here, by the way,' Anna said. 'Hand on heart. Abso-blooming-lutely!'

Rachel giggled. 'I like the way you say that.'

In a gap in the traffic, we went to cross the road.

'Let me get my breath back a sec,' Anna wheezed, waving us on. 'I'll catch you up.'

I was a bit wary about going on without her. But Ray's wristwatch said it was now almost dead on half past nine. The seaside bus would be leaving. And sure enough, as we ran through the station entrance, the green double decker was already pulling away from its stand.

'Hey!' Ray shrieked. 'Wait for us!'

'Stop!' I yelled, waving my arms above my head.

Rachel, who was fast on her feet, ran after the bus

till she was almost alongside it. Ray and me tried again to wave it down. But the doors were closed, the driver staring stony-faced at the road ahead. I couldn't believe we'd missed our ride by seconds. It was so infuriating, I almost burst into tears on the spot, which I didn't suppose would help anyone. To make matters worse, it had started to rain rather heavily.

'Now what?' Ray asked, taking his annoyance out on the kerb by kicking it.

'Well, I'm not going into school,' Rachel said, very definitely.

'Me neither,' I agreed. 'Not for grammar lessons.'

Ray stopped kicking to look up and around.

'Oh no,' he said, in a way that made my stomach drop. 'Where's Anna?'

She wasn't where we'd left her, on the other side of the road. I couldn't see her inside the station, either. The place was filling up with people. More buses were arriving. Passengers were getting on and off.

'She must be here somewhere,' I groaned.

'We'll check by the entrance.' Ray beckoned Rachel to go with him.

I checked the bus queues, the people sheltering under umbrellas. I was beginning to get frantic, when I noticed Ray at the bus station entrance.

'Stevie! We've found her!' he yelled.

Massively relieved, I ran over to join them. The double decker had stopped just outside the station, at the junction with the main road. The door at the rear was open. Someone in purple corduroy trousers was talking to the bus conductor.

Anna.

I arrived just in time to catch the tail end of what appeared to be a very theatrical speech.

'Sea swimming's the only cure, so the doctors have told me,' she was explaining. 'It's my last hope, and if it doesn't work for me, then . . .' She trailed off so mournfully, the bus conductor had to wipe his eyes.

I didn't believe a word of what she was saying, yet the conductor was completely taken in.

'On you get then, love. These your pals?' The man turned to us. 'Come on, let's be having you.'

Thanking him, and grinning slyly at each other, we piled on board.

'You were brilliant,' I whispered to Anna.

'That was some performance,' Rachel agreed, clearly in awe.

'Poor man, though,' Ray muttered. 'I hope he's not too upset.'

I nudged Ray. 'You're such a softie, you are!'

'Ha! Not always.' He had such a cheeky look on his face, I couldn't help but laugh.

Once we'd got our tickets, we tried to find seats but the bus was so crowded we had to stand for the first few stops. I didn't care a jot. We held on to seats and ceiling straps and, as I caught Ray's eye over the top of people's heads, I kept grinning. We'd done it! We were on our way to the seaside!

The bus passed through town, more and more people getting off, and very few getting on. Seats emptied, aisles cleared. We really wanted to sit upstairs, at the front, where you could see everything and it felt as if you were perched on a cliff edge. And, at the final town centre stop, once the last passengers had clattered down the stairs, we raced up to claim our spot. The two pairs of double seats right in front were ours.

'This is the best,' Rachel declared, settling into her seat next to Ray.

'You're not really going to swim in the sea today, like you told the bus conductor, are you?' I asked Anna, as we took the left-hand seats.

Anna didn't answer. The bus had stopped at traffic lights, and she wiped the misted-up glass with her sleeve and lowered her sunglasses, distracted by something outside.

'That building there, the big one with all the windows. Is that the hospital?' she wanted to know.

The building was a huge grey box, five or six storeys high and wet as a whale's back in the rain.

'Yup, that's it,' I confirmed.

There were lawns and flower beds all around the hospital, and paths lined with signposts filled with very long words, most of which ended in 'ology', though I recognised a few like 'X-ray' and 'Children's Ward'. The hospital had been open a couple of years and everyone said it was a good thing for our town.

'It's where Stevie's mum works,' Rachel told her.

Anna pulled a sour face. 'Ugh, your poor mum. I hate hospitals.'

'At least this one's local,' I said, defensively. 'When my dad was sick we had to travel miles to see him at the hospital.' The endless buses and trains, and waiting around on cold, wet platforms, the total boredom of it all, stuck in my head almost as much as him being ill.

'Hmmm, I s'pose,' Anna replied.

She didn't say any more about hospitals or ask why Dad was in one, and I was glad: I didn't want to talk about it, either. It was a relief when the traffic lights turned green, and the bus moved on.

Another five minutes of houses, bungalows, a garage,

and we'd left town behind us altogether. As the road straightened out, we picked up speed. The houses became fields, the walls and garden fences rows of trees in autumn colours that seemed even brighter because of the rain. Rachel passed round a bag of pear drops. They were sticky and had to be prised apart, but tasted good.

'You're glad I came now, aren't you? Go on, admit it,' Rachel said.

'Don't push your luck, shorty,' Ray answered, but his arm was tucked affectionately through hers.

'What shall we do when we get to Budmouth Point?' I asked. We had money to spend, after all. Anna's trouser pocket was bulging with the change from our bus tickets.

'Anna's made her mind up already – she's going swimming,' Rachel answered.

Anna didn't reply. She'd fallen asleep, her head leaning against the window. I hadn't noticed the sore places in the corners of her mouth before. It was probably the first time I'd seen her this close up in full daylight.

I turned to Ray. 'What do you want to do today? Going to America is out of the question, obviously, but . . .'

Ray sighed, like he'd remembered something.

'What?' I asked.

'Just thinking about my cousin Violet's latest letter.'

'What did she say about the missile business?'

'I haven't had a chance to read it yet.'

'He's been distracted.' Rachel grinned. 'Pete has been too – because *he's* got a new girlfriend.'

'What the heck's *that* got to do with anything?' Ray cried, throwing up his arms in exasperation.

I couldn't help laughing. 'Oh, your face, Ray! It's hilarious!'

He pretended to be shocked, which made me laugh even more. Rachel, who was brilliant at impressions, then did one of her mum. She got the voice exactly right – stern and a bit scary, but kind.

'*Pete, why don't you ask your young lady round for tea? Even better, she can join us in the bunker!*'

Ray groaned. 'Oh no, not the bunker, that's not funny.'

'I'm more interested in Pete's girlfriend,' I remarked. 'Any idea who she is yet?'

As no one seemed to know, we came up with a few likely contenders, which got steadily more ridiculous till our list had on it Queen Elizabeth, Princess Margaret and Mrs Talbot from the paper shop. At one point, the nice bus conductor came upstairs to ask us to keep the noise down, because the other passengers were complaining. Amazingly, Anna slept through it all.

Once we'd run out of girlfriends for Pete, we played a

silly version of I Spy where we could only choose things that started with the letter P. The weather had worsened so it was a job to see anything much, other than brown moorland and bedraggled sheep.

'We're crossing Dartmoor, that's why,' Ray said, going into 'information mode'. 'This road's pretty high up. I bet you it gets blocked by snow in the winter.'

Today it was rain that kept falling. The windows on each side of the bus were steamed up, and the windscreen in front of us was running with water. Against our shins the heating vents pumped out warm air. Usually, I hated bus rides, but I felt so giddily happy, I didn't want this one to end.

Eventually it did, though. The road swooped down towards the sea, and Ray, leaping from his seat like he'd just sat on a wasp, shouted, 'I spy the lighthouse!'

It didn't start with the letter P, but we forgave him.

15

I'd been expecting a sleepy fishing village, with cobbled streets and white-painted cottages, because that was how Budmouth Point looked in Ray's holiday snaps. In real life it was a bustling little town with a grocer's, a butcher's shop with a queue outside, and a place that sold shoes and vacuum cleaners. As we got off the bus, I was also convinced it was the windiest place on earth.

'Is it always like this?' I yelled, trying – and failing – to zip up my anorak. The wind was blustering straight from the sea, almost blowing me back into the road.

'Pretty much!' Ray shouted. 'You wait till we get down to the beach!'

Already I could hear the roar of the sea, and taste salt on my lips. The main street went steeply downhill, taking us past a building with steps outside that Ray said had once been the post office his mum's family owned. It was now a shop selling beach balls and postcards. In the window, a fat ginger cat lay asleep, until Rachel tapped on the glass.

'Hello, Treacle,' she cooed as the cat lifted its head. 'He remembers me from the summer, look.'

I didn't see much evidence: the cat thumped its tail, then went back to sleep.

'Give me dogs, any day,' I remarked.

Huddling out of the wind in the shop doorway, we set about deciding what to do first.

'Can we get chips?' Rachel begged. 'I'm starving.'

'You always are.' Ray gave her a chocolate bar from his back pocket that looked as if it had been sat on for the entire bus ride.

'I don't mind what we do,' I said. I was just glad to be away from World's End Close. For the first time all week, I felt properly unknotted, as light-hearted as if we actually were here on our holidays.

'How about the lighthouse?' Anna suggested, yawning herself awake. 'That's it, down there, isn't it?'

At the end of the street, glimpsed between the rooftops, was what appeared to be a huge glass lantern, hovering in the sky. I'd never seen a real lighthouse before. We all agreed it was worth closer look.

Back out in the full blast of the wind, we headed down to the harbour. Here the street ended in a wide cobbled path that ran to the foot of the lighthouse. To the left of it was the main beach, to the right the harbour itself, which was, thankfully, more sheltered. All the fishing boats were in today – because of the weather, Ray said – and they jostled in the water, rasping and bumping against each other, as the gulls screeched overhead.

'Bet they're hungry enough to peck your eyes out,' Ray said, swooping down on Rachel.

She squealed so loudly that Anna, laughing, put her fingers in her ears. I wasn't paying much attention, already lost to the lighthouse.

'Woweee!' I tilted my head back to take in the view.

The lighthouse was like something out of a storybook. It was perfectly round, red-and-white striped, with little windows at intervals all the way up. Alarmingly, the front door was at least twenty feet off the ground. To reach it you had to climb an iron ladder that clung to the side of the building. On a day like today, when the waves were big and foamy, it looked terrifying.

'Is that the only way in and out?' I asked Ray.

''Course it is.'

'But people actually *live* in there, don't they?' I said, remembering what he'd once told me. 'Your parents know them. They've got two boys – twins you can't tell apart?'

'Yup. Ephraim's the lighthouse keeper, married to Sukie, who writes books.'

'Slushy, yucky romance books,' Rachel said, wrinkling her nose in a way that made her look just like Ray.

'That sell in their millions all around the world,' Ray reminded her. 'Plus, Sukie's really nice.'

'She is,' Rachel agreed. 'Though the twins are a right pair of numpties.'

I was still amazed by the ladder to the front door. 'When they go to school, or the shops, or whatever, they have to go up and down it?'

'Sure they do,' Ray insisted. 'And the dogs: they've been trained to climb it.'

The thought of Flea scrabbling up a ladder, twenty feet above the waves, made me clutch my stomach.

'Hell, I'd never let a dog of mine do that,' Anna agreed.

'No one's ever fallen off,' Ray pointed out. 'Human *or* dog.'

'Are we going to say hello to Sukie?' Rachel then asked.

'Better not. She'll be writing, and it's bad form to disturb authors when they're at work.'

Rachel rolled her eyes. 'Just because *you* get grumpy when you're writing stories, doesn't mean everyone does.'

Still, faced with that ladder, I was very happy not to call in – or up – or however you visited someone who lived in a lighthouse.

*

After we'd done a brisk lap of the harbour, we doubled back for the beach. It wasn't a cold day – the sky had cleared and the sun was now out – but the wind was still so fierce you could lean into it as you walked. Not that it bothered anyone. We were all in high spirits, chatting and giggling, and taking it in turns to try on Anna's sunglasses.

'We could be queueing up for our school dinner now,' I reminded Ray.

It was his turn with the sunglasses: he lowered them in sudden shock. 'I've not thought about school – not once! Have you?'

'Nope. Or the war.'

'Hey, don't start now,' Anna warned.

I hadn't forgotten our one rule.

As we jumped down on to the beach, I unzipped my anorak and flipped it over my head and shoulders.

'Watch this,' I said.

Kids did it all the time in the playground at

school – the wind caught your coat like a sail and if you got it just right, it'd almost blow you off your feet. I turned my coat-sail to the wind and ran. A huge gust pushed me forward so fast my stomach flew up with it. My feet nearly left the ground. By the time the wind dropped again, I was twenty yards down the beach.

When I looked back at the others, Ray was waving his arms and yelling, 'Whoa! That was the business!'

'You're like Batman!' Anna cried.

Rachel hammered down the beach towards me, struggling to hold her coat above her head. The others followed on behind. Ray, like me, having done it loads at school, managed to get his coat-sail up, and was blown almost down to the sea's edge. Anna gave up after the first attempt.

'My outfit's all wrong!' she wailed, plucking at her heavy winter coat.

I offered her my anorak.

'Nah, you're all right,' she said.

She looked tired still, I thought, dark under the eyes. I wondered if it was time for us to have some lunch.

With this in mind, we wandered back along the beach towards town. Ray was in front, chatting over his shoulder about where we could get chips.

'He should look where he's going,' Rachel sniggered.

Almost instantly, he went over. A flurry of legs. Pebbles. And the funniest slow-motion slide down the beach on to the wet sand where the tide had come in. He lay in a heap, groaning. I felt guilty for laughing so hard, until Rachel told us, 'It's his party trick. He does it every summer.'

Since he was wet already, Ray announced he might as well go for a quick paddle. He took off his shoes and socks, rolled up his school trousers.

'Wait for us!' I cried, because if we'd come all the way to the seaside we simply *had* to go in the water.

At first the sea was so cold it made my feet go numb.

'It'll be warmer if we run in,' Rachel reckoned, grabbing my hand.

Of course, it wasn't. But shrieking about it made it funnier. Then Ray started splashing us.

'That's for calling me a softie earlier, on the bus!' he cried, scooping up water in both hands.

'I was only joking!' I yelped.

'Let's get him back,' Rachel decided.

We'd almost got into a full-scale water fight, when I noticed Anna hadn't joined us. She was sitting on the beach near our shoes, chin on knees, trailing her hand over the pebbles.

I waved. 'You coming in? It's not that cold, really.'

'It's the magic cure,' Rachel called to her. 'That's what you said to the bus conductor man.'

Anna looked up, smiled. 'Don't tell him I didn't go in, will you?'

Having had enough of the sea myself, I hobbled back up the beach. The others came too, and we sat with Anna, dusting off our feet and putting our shoes and socks on again.

'I think coming here is a magic cure,' Rachel said wistfully, then noticed Anna laughing. '*What?*'

'You, getting all soppy,' Anna teased.

'Well, I love it here,' said Ray, who wouldn't mind being thought soppy. 'It's a special place.'

I sat back, staring over the golden shingle and out across the sea as it churned around the lighthouse. The view seemed familiar. 'Was this the *actual* beach where your mum rescued those people?' I asked, because it looked like the same spot as in the photograph on their living-room wall.

'Yup.' Ray grew thoughtful. 'The first mission was February 1941, and they did it a few more times after that.'

'What did your mum do, Ray?' Anna asked, looking at him with new interest.

'In the last war, she rescued people running away from

Hitler. Her and her friends did it in secret, smuggling people into the country,' he explained. 'They got into trouble for it – the coastguard dobbed them in – but that didn't stop them.'

'I'm named after one of the women who helped,' Rachel added proudly. 'You might not guess it from looking at our mum, but she saved a lot of lives.'

This was the Mrs Johnson I'd seen yesterday in Ray's kitchen, arguing over the airbase bunker. It was a quiet, determined sort of bravery, not the comic-book, superhero kind.

'Runs in the family, does it, helping runaways?' Anna said, a twinkle in her eye.

Ray shrugged. 'Maybe.'

I didn't really see the connection, myself. What Mrs Johnson did in the war took incredible courage, while all we'd done was help one girl. In fact, sitting here on the beach, laughing and chatting, when we could've been at school, worrying, it was almost as if Anna was the one rescuing us, not the other way around.

16

Since it was too windy for eating chips outside, Ray took us to a cafe called Bagatelli's. The lady behind the counter did a double take when she saw Ray and Rachel.

'If it isn't my two favourite Johnsons!' she cried, her accent American like Ray's dad's. 'Not on vacation again, are you, huh?'

She was wearing a badge on her apron that said: *Your waitress today is Vera*.

'Hi, Vera.' Ray shot Rachel a quick warning look that said *he'd* do the talking. 'Just a day trip this time with our friends.'

For one awkward second, I worried Vera was going to ask where Ray's parents were and why we weren't in school. But, all she did was give us a huge, pink-lipsticked smile, and showed us to our seats.

The cafe was so tiny there were only three tables, each one already set with white plates, cutlery, bottles of ketchup and vinegar. Rock 'n' roll music was playing on a jukebox in the corner. The air smelled sugary sweet, like candyfloss at a fairground. The menu was full of exciting stuff like beefburgers, cheeseburgers, chips, milkshakes, cream sodas.

'Bet you love it in here,' I said to Ray. 'It feels so American!'

He grinned. 'Dad says it's the closest to an American diner he's ever seen since living over here.'

On the jukebox, the music suddenly changed.

'A-WOP-BOP-A-LOO-BOP-A-LOP-BOMP-BOMP . . .'

'Little Richard!' Rachel jumped to her feet. 'I love this song!'

Ray groaned. 'Oh no, she's going to dance, isn't she?'

But he was only pretending: from the moment Rachel started jiving, it was obvious she was brilliant.

'TUTTI FRUTTI, AW RUTTI . . .'

My foot started tapping. It was such a catchy song you couldn't hear it and sit still. Last time it'd been on the radio at home, Mum and Bev tried to dance to it, and were totally rubbish. Rachel was in a whole different league. Despite the lack of space between the tables, her flicks and kicks were so fast it hardly mattered. I couldn't take my eyes off her.

'Come on!' Rachel pulled Anna to her feet. 'I'll teach you.'

But the music was so fast, Anna was soon breathless.

'I can't do it!' she cried, falling back in her seat.

The music changed again. This time it was 'Jailhouse Rock' by Elvis Presley.

'Hear that?' Ray said, making us listen to the song, which sounded thin, somehow, compared to the previous one. 'That's what Pete means when he says Elvis isn't the true king.'

*

When Vera came back to our table with burger-filled plates balanced up her arms, I wondered how we'd ever eat it all. My cheeseburger alone was the size of a football. Biting into it made me think of those snakes that dislocate their jaws so they can eat a goat whole. We had chips too – thin ones, called *fries*. For afters it was chocolate sundae, though Ray had a float, which was cola with ice cream on top.

Half an hour later, our table was a sea of greasy plates and empty glasses, dollops of ketchup and melted cheese. I felt sick. Rachel kept burping, and Anna was yawning again.

'How many of these film stars do you recognise?' Ray asked, pointing to the photos covering the walls.

It was a question for Anna, really, as the big movie fan among us. But she'd gone very quiet, her head slumped forward, as if she was nodding off to sleep.

'Easy,' I said, answering. 'That's Marilyn Monroe, and that one . . .' I hesitated at a man in a white T-shirt, whose quiffed-up hair was like Pete's.

'James Dean,' Ray confirmed. 'And the man with the cap on the motorbike, that's Marlon Brando. Next to him is Sophia Loren.'

The names didn't mean much to me, but Rachel, face in hands, gave a dreamy sigh. 'They're my heroes.'

'Maybe your picture'll be up there one day, when you're famous,' I told her.

'Maybe,' Ray said, rather gloomily I thought. 'Though I bet it's as much about looks as talent.'

'Don't they have black film stars?' I asked, thinking I'd seen that Sidney Poitier chap in Ray's scrapbook of important Americans.

'Not many, no.'

From the number of white faces on the walls, it was obvious, and I felt stupid for asking. The same thing had happened with our school play, hadn't it, when Mr Reilly gave Rachel such a tiny part despite her talent. No wonder she'd been upset, and Mr Johnson had wanted to speak to the school.

There was one photo of a black man here, though, which Ray was now looking at.

'See this man?' He lifted his chin at the picture that hung above the coffee machine. It was of a man in a shirt and tie, standing in front of an enormous crowd. 'He's Dr Martin Luther King, Junior. Remember his name.'

'He's not a movie star, is he?' I asked, recalling Ray saying how he wanted to meet him one day.

'No. He's fighting for equal rights for black people in America. He's incredible – my cousin Violet's told me all about him. However brutal the police and government are, he wants people to fight back peacefully, with words.'

'Speaking out, you mean?'

'Yeah, and going on peaceful protests, I suppose, marches or sit-ins. Like Rosa Parks refusing to give up her bus seat for a white person.'

I nodded: Bev had told me Rosa Parks's story. And the idea of taking a stand, quietly and peacefully, sounded a bit like what Dad had said in his letter.

'Dr King gives incredible speeches. Violet reckons he's got the sort of voice you can't help but listen to. Look at this crowd.' Ray indicated the photo. 'I bet there's thousands here who've come to hear him speak.'

I stared at Dr King. Anyone who could get up and

speak in front of so many people was a total hero in my eyes.

*

After the diner, in need of fresh air, we wandered back down to the sea. On the beach, a couple of dogs were chasing sticks, and we leaned on the seafront railings to watch them.

'Should've brought Flea,' I said. 'She'd love it here.'

Ray chuckled. 'Geez, can't you live without dogs for one day?'

'Why should she, though?' Anna retorted. 'Say this *was* Stevie's last day on earth? Her wish was to spend the day with a hundred dogs, wasn't it?'

'Yeah.' I smiled. 'Not likely to happen, though. I mean, Ray's wish was to go to America—'

'– hence Bagatelli's,' he pointed out.

'Mine was to have a bath and see the sea.' Anna gestured to her clean clothes, the beach. 'Which I've done.'

'So?' I answered warily.

'Could you manage one hundred *and one* dogs? Because I think I've worked out where the cinema is.' She pointed back up the hill to the street just past the diner, then checked her watch again. 'The film starts in fifteen minutes.'

'A film?' Rachel beamed. 'Who's in it?'

'Dogs, mostly,' Ray warned her.

But I knew which movie Anna meant, even before I saw the cinema poster, with its cartoon Dalmatian dogs and the leering black-and-white-haired villain. I'd been wanting to see *One Hundred and One Dalmatians* for ages. Ray, who'd read the book, said the story was ace.

'Oh, Anna, it's . . . I mean . . . thank you,' I stuttered.

Because she'd done this for me.

*

Like all good things, the day finally came to an end, and we caught the bus home. Anna rested her head on my shoulder and promptly fell asleep. She smelled of the popcorn we'd eaten at the cinema. Her woolly hat prickled against my neck, as I mulled happily over my favourite parts of the day: the lighthouse, charging down the beach with our coats over our heads, the cheeseburgers. Or maybe Rachel dancing the jive, or watching *One Hundred and One Dalmatians* in the dark and coming out again to find it was still daylight. There were so many to choose from. And if this really did turn out to be our last day on earth, then we'd certainly had a whole lot of fun.

The lull of the bus eventually sent me off to sleep too. I woke some time later to Ray tapping me on the arm.

'We're just coming into town, Vie,' he warned.

I sat up, gave my stiff neck a rub, glanced out of the window. We'd stopped outside the hospital.

'What time is it?' I asked Ray.

He looked at his watch. 'Nearly seven.'

For the first time all day, I let myself think about home – Bev worrying, Nan annoyed because the plate of dinner she'd have kept warm in the oven was going dry. A surge of guilt came over me. I was going to be in trouble for this. Big trouble.

As the bus stopped again, more people, bags, umbrellas got on, bringing with them the damp, evening air. Two women who took the seats across from us started to chat about the news.

'It's wise to prepare ourselves.' The woman speaking had a shopping bag on her lap. 'Last time we had a war, I couldn't get a decent cauliflower for love or money.'

'Do you really think they'll do it, either of them?' Her friend tapped the evening newspaper she'd been reading. On the front page were two photos – one of handsome

Mr Kennedy, the other of jowly faced Mr Khrushchev, the Russian leader – positioned to make it look like the men were glaring straight at each other.

'Well, it'll only take one of them to press a button and that'll be it,' the shopping-bag woman replied. 'I expect we'll soon find out when those Russian ships reach Cuba.'

'When are they due to get there?'

'Some time tomorrow, so I've heard.'

I tried not to listen. But the women's voices were persistent, as was the feeling of dread seeping through me. All day I'd told myself not to think bad thoughts – that had been our rule and it had worked, mostly. Yet I was reminded now of Bev and me moving the bedroom wardrobe, how just one little movement had brought everything crashing down.

Kennedy and Khrushchev still hated each other. War was on the cards. Anna was being followed by people who wanted to harm her. In the hours we'd been somewhere else, feeling happy, nothing had really changed.

*

The walk home from the bus station seemed to take forever. It was cold and raining. We were tired, each of us, and not looking forward to what we were about to face. We also needed to get our story straight.

'What are we going to say when they ask where we've been?' I said to Ray.

'The truth – it's probably easier than lying.'

'No mention of me,' Anna reminded us.

For someone who'd slept a fair bit today, she looked proper, sunken-eyed, done-in tired. It crossed my mind that she might be getting ill – the flu or something – because it was pretty damp up in that pillbox. The farmer worried me too, with his threats to shoot things. Maybe it wasn't quite such a perfect hiding place after all.

'Whoa! Look!' Suddenly, Ray flung his arm out like a barrier, making us stop dead on the pavement.

A car was parked outside Ray's house, the words POLICE in big black lettering on its side.

'Oh crikey,' I breathed. This was worse than I thought: Mrs Johnson must've reported us missing. Now we were *officially* in trouble.

'We'd better go.' Ray took his sister's hand. 'Just tell the truth, remember: we bunked off school, went to the seaside, had burgers and watched a film.'

'Because we were worried about the war and wanted a bit of fun,' I said, though I didn't reckon the grown-ups would think much of our excuse, somehow.

With Ray and Rachel gone, Anna and me walked together as far as the gap in the houses. 'I'll find my way back to the pillbox from here,' she said, with a quick goodbye.

'Just a sec.' I stopped her.

Maybe it was us being alone for the first time all day, but suddenly, my other question, the one I'd been waiting for the right moment to ask, came tumbling out of my mouth.

'How d'you know my surname? And coming here, to World's End Close, how did you know it even existed?'

'*What?*' Anna took a step back, hands on head, bewildered.

'You dropped your notebook last night. It's written on the inside cover. I've got it upstairs.' I glanced towards the house as I said it. 'I know you hate questions but it's been bugging me all—'

When I turned back to her, I was talking to the darkness. Anna had gone.

17

By now, I was very late home: *three whole hours* and counting. The telling-off of a lifetime was coming my way, I knew it, and as I walked up our front path, bracing myself, I had a sudden, painful pang for Mum. At least her tellings-off were short and to the point: I wasn't sure how badly Nan was going to react.

The second I set foot indoors, Flea hurled herself at me, a frenzy of tongue and tail. Nan and Bev were seated at the table.

'Oh, there you are, Stevie love!' Nan gushed. Then to Bev, stating the obvious, rather, 'Here she is, look!'

The friendly greeting threw me completely. As did the fact they were playing Monopoly again, this time without bickering. Everything else was as it always was – the stove was warm, the washing-up drying on the draining board, the smell of dinner lingering. Bev was still in her school uniform – minus the tie – Nan wearing a blue jumper that on its own would've been quite normal, but she'd added an orange scarf and a brooch that looked like a giant eagle's claw. The police hadn't been round here yet, that was becoming obvious, but I knew they would be, just as soon as they'd finished at Ray's.

'Hi, sorry I'm late,' I muttered, stooping down to stroke Flea, so I didn't have to meet anyone's eye.

Nan got up. Taking still-warm beef stew and roast potatoes from the oven, she cleared a place for me at the table.

'Thought you'd be famished, pet,' she said, putting a heaped plate in front of me. 'Go on, dig in.'

Despite being full up from the burger, I thought it best to show willing and picked up my knife and fork. And *still* no one asked me where I'd been and why I was so late home. I was beginning to think I'd somehow got away with it. But when Nan went to the larder to fetch bread and butter, Bev was on to me like a shot.

'I saw you catch that bus this morning,' she whispered fiercely.

My fork froze halfway to my mouth. The bus station was opposite the grammar school – it hadn't occurred to me that Bev, of all people, might've seen us.

'It's okay.' Bev's whisper softened a little. 'I told Nan you were staying at school late.'

I gulped. 'Errr . . . thanks.'

But it wasn't me I was most worried about. If Bev had spotted us today, she'd also have seen Anna. I pushed my plate away, feeling slightly sick.

Luckily, we were out of bread, and Nan was more interested in playing Monopoly, anyway.

'I was just about to buy Fleet Street,' she said, taking her seat. 'But shall we start the game again now Stevie's back?'

'Good idea,' I agreed.

Glad of the distraction, I carried my plate over to the sink. I really couldn't eat a thing. Whenever we played Monopoly my piece was always the Scottie dog. It was as Bev passed it to me that I noticed the bandage on her hand.

'What happened to you?' I asked.

'Your sister got the cane, that's what,' Nan answered curtly. 'All for having an opinion about these stupid missiles in Cuba.'

Bev's schoolbag lay open next to her chair, her 'Ban the Bomb' posters inside, some still rolled up neatly, others all crumpled as if she'd stuffed them away in a hurry.

'You did it, then? The protest?' I asked.

'We certainly did.' Unlike Nan, Bev was smiling. 'In the dining hall, at lunchtime. Ten of us from the sixth form, plus some of the younger girls.'

'Wow, Bev! That's super brilliant!'

'Ah, well.' She shrugged, all modest for once. 'We should really have done a speech or something, but none of us had the guts for that.'

'You're still brave, though,' I pointed out, glancing at her hand. 'Did the cane hurt?'

'A bit.' Bev flexed her fingers. Winced. 'Girls get done by a female teacher – makes it fairer, apparently.' She rolled her eyes at this. 'Though I'm sure she did it doubly hard, on purpose.'

Still, I was in awe. And when I compared what Bev and her pals had done to our day at the seaside, the shine began to come off it, rather. Maybe we should've done something bigger and bolder, that would've made a difference not just to us but to everyone. Perhaps we'd feel better if we'd done something more *purposeful*, like Bev with her school protest.

'Well, honestly,' Nan huffed, not yet finished on the subject of Bev's punishment. 'What do they expect clever girls to do, eh? This is your future you're standing up for. Your dad fought those Nazis, and if he was here now, he'd still be fighting for what's right.'

It was a bit different from what she'd said when she first arrived. Bev had impressed her, I could tell.

'We've not given up, don't worry.' With her good hand

Bev reached down into her bag and pulled out a flyer that said 'March for Peace' on it. 'We're protesting through town tomorrow and hoping for a real crowd. Starts at two o'clock by the war memorial. Everyone's welcome. You both should come.'

'I will,' I said straight off. Then I considered Ray. Would he want to come? A few days ago I wouldn't have thought it likely, what with his dad being an American who worked at the airbase, readying all those planes for action against the Russians.

And now? Now he'd read Dad's letter. He'd disagreed with his parents' nuclear shelter plan. He'd even bunked a day off school.

'I'll ask Ray,' I promised. 'He told me about this American man called Dr King who says peaceful protests are the way to get people to listen.'

Bev's face lit up. 'Yes! Dr Martin Luther King – he's speaking out against segregation in America, isn't he?'

I nodded, pleased to know something my sister approved of.

'And what about Mum? She's back tomorrow, isn't she?' Bev asked Nan.

'Don't count on it,' Nan replied gloomily. 'They've said on the radio that the trains are far busier than normal. I suppose everyone's trying to get home, just in case,' her hand went to her throat, 'the worst happens.'

I felt a prickle of panic. A nuclear bomb would wipe out roads, train lines. It could take Mum weeks to get home – if she made it back at all. Suddenly, all I wanted was for our house to be full of noise again, for pop songs on the radio and Mum clattering about the kitchen, or upstairs taking ages in the bath. I didn't even mind that she hadn't hugged me goodbye before she'd left. I just missed her and wished she'd come home.

'Don't worry,' Bev said, seeing my face. 'It'll be—'

She was interrupted by a hammering on our front door.

'Haven't they heard of doorbells?' Nan moaned, getting up to answer it.

When she came back to the kitchen, it was with a man in a navy-blue police uniform. I'd known this was coming the second we'd seen his car parked outside Ray's. Yet now the moment was here, the story we'd all agreed on escaped me. I felt tongue-tied.

'This is Sergeant Mukherjee, girls.' Nan did the introductions, then offered the policeman a seat and some tea.

'No, thank you, ma'am.' Sergeant Mukherjee stayed standing. This made me more nervous, because in television shows like *Z-Cars* if a policeman didn't sit down it usually meant he was proper tough, or that he had terrible news to share.

Even then, I wasn't ready for what he told us.

'We're trying to locate a missing girl,' he explained. 'We're calling at every house in the neighbourhood as part of our enquiries. The girl's parents are new to the street, and have reported her missing since Tuesday.'

My first thought was relief. So this *wasn't* about us bunking off school.

'*This* street?' Nan's eyes glittered with interest. 'They'll be the new neighbours at number two, won't they?'

'That's right.' Sergeant Mukherjee nodded.

'The Burgesses,' I murmured, thinking of the paper I'd delivered there this morning, and the sound of crying coming from inside.

'Keeping an eye out at the kitchen window comes in handy,' Nan said in a smug aside to us, then politely to the policeman, 'Her poor parents must be worried to death.'

'They are,' Sergeant Mukherjee agreed. 'She's been gone a good few days now. They tried to track her down themselves, and hoped she would return of her own accord, but she hasn't, which is why we've stepped in.'

'She's run away from home, then?' Bev wanted to know.

'Something like that,' the policeman replied cagily.

The heat was building in my face. I knew exactly who they were talking about. A girl running away from home, known to be in this area? How often did that happen in a neighbourhood like ours?

'What can we do to help, sergeant?' Nan asked.

'Stay alert,' he advised. 'Let us know if you see anything suspicious.'

It was easier just to keep my eyes on the Monopoly board, and hope Sergeant Mukherjee would hurry up and go. Maybe it wasn't Anna he was talking about, I told myself, because he hadn't mentioned her by name. I held on to this small possibility, until he took a photograph from his inside pocket and laid it on the table.

'If you see anyone fitting this description, please get in touch straight away,' he said.

It was one of those home-Polaroid snaps, with 'Anna, Christmas 1961' written underneath in biro. The girl in the picture was almost as tall as the Christmas tree she stood beside. She wasn't skinny like the Anna we knew, and she had thick, dark, plaited hair. But it was unmistakably her.

'Poor thing. Hope she's okay.' Bev sighed. 'She must've had a fight with her parents or something.'

That wasn't how Anna had put it: she'd told us she

was hiding from people who were trying to *poison* her with arsenic. It might not have been the whole story, exactly, but there was no mistaking how scared she'd been. I'd seen it first-hand. Anna desperately didn't want to be found.

'I'm not at liberty to discuss the finer details, I'm afraid,' Sergeant Mukherjee replied.

How much did the police know about Anna, I wondered?

And the dreaded truth of it: how much did *we* know?

A few new things, it seemed, thanks to the policeman's visit: her surname, and where her parents lived, and possibly the reason she'd known about World's End Close: because her family were planning to move here.

*

Once Sergeant Mukherjee had gone, Bev hauled me, very determinedly, upstairs. Shutting our bedroom door and leaning against it, she said: 'You'd better tell me what's going on, Stevie.'

'What d'you mean?' I tried to bluff.

'I *saw* you, remember? You, Ray, Rachel, and a tall girl wearing *my* yellow jumper and Mum's sunglasses.'

I sat down on my sister's bed. I had no choice but to trust Bev. Wiping my sweaty palms on my knees, I started from the beginning.

*

Later, Nan came in with hot-water bottles and Horlicks, telling us not to worry because the poor missing girl would soon be found. Once she'd gone to bed, Bev turned to me, tucking her hair behind her ears in a way that meant business.

'Right, Vie,' she said briskly. 'What're you going to do about all this?'

I blew on my Horlicks. What could we do – tell the police about the arsenic poisoners? Tell Anna to leave? Go across the road and speak to her parents ourselves?

In the end Bev, impatient for an answer, reckoned I should start by talking to Ray and Anna.

'The police know the area. They're bound to check the pillbox if they haven't already,' she added. 'Get Anna away from here tonight if you can.'

'*Tonight?*'

'Maybe wait five minutes till Nan's asleep. But do it now. You'll regret it if you don't.'

She was right, as usual. Too many people were now

on Anna's trail. And the tricky part was knowing who to fear most – the poisoners or the police who wanted her to go home.

18

The pillbox was in darkness when I got there. Over to my left, the airbase fence buzzed menacingly; beyond it, the runway stretched long and silent, like an animal waiting to pounce.

Inside, the pillbox smelled damp and cold.

'Anna?' I called, in case she was hiding. 'It's Stevie. It's all right, I'm on my own.'

There was no answer. The air felt still, another indication she wasn't here. I tried to think where she might've gone – a walk, maybe? Unlikely, when she'd been so tired all day.

The other option made my heart sink: the reality was she might've already left. And why wouldn't she, when the police were closing in?

In the time I'd been at home, she could easily have made it back to Havana Road, to have another go at fetching whatever it was she'd come here for – *whoever* she'd come for. She could be miles away by now. Perhaps we'd never see Anna again. But I wasn't ready to think about that.

Torch on, I did a quick search of the pillbox. There were signs she'd been back here tonight – since the bus ride home, anyway. Bev's yellow jumper lay on top of the sleeping bag, the sunglasses next to it. And in a shiny heap on the pillow, the loose change left over from our seaside trip. It made me sad, seeing all those things together. Despite our marvellous day out, the difficult stuff hadn't gone away; I'd learned that today, as well.

*

At Ray's all the lights were out, which was encouraging because it meant the Johnsons were in bed. Ray's room was at the rear of the house, so I went down the side alley to the back gate. It occurred to me how, just a few nights ago, he'd been the one throwing stones at my bedroom window: now it was my turn to wake him. There was just enough yellowy light from the street lamps to see where I was going. My hand was on the gate latch when I heard something – someone – marching towards me from the opposite end of the alley. Instantly, I recognised the silhouetted bobble hat, the long, spindly legs.

'Anna!' I gasped, almost laughing with relief.

She stopped in front of me. Her overcoat buttons glinted in the dark like four pairs of fierce, silvery eyes.

'What are you doing here?' she whispered.

I was getting the distinct feeling that *she* wasn't glad to see me.

'Looking for you. I thought you'd already gone,' I tried to explain.

'I *am* going.'

'Without saying goodbye?'

Anna tried to look cool, in control: the giveaway was her chin, which was trembling.

'Look.' She sniffed. 'I'm not very good at farewells, okay?'

Nor was I, I suddenly realised. Should we hug? Swap addresses? It was actually easier just to keep talking.

'Where *are* you going?' I asked, because I thought now, finally, she might just give me a proper answer.

Anna patted her coat pocket in a way that seemed to mean something, though I wasn't sure what. 'To do one more thing, which'll hopefully be easier than it was the last time I tried.'

'I meant where are you going for good?'

She hesitated. She didn't want to tell me, even then, and after all we'd done together, it really stung. I held up my hands, disappointed. Defeated.

'All right, no ruddy quest—'

'To Wales,' Anna interrupted. 'It's where my favourite aunt lives. She's always inviting me to go and stay. And I *do* trust you, you know. I trust you and Ray more than anyone.'

'Oh.' Slowly, I took in what she was saying: a straight answer, at last, and proof that Ray and me had earned her friendship. I felt crazily pleased.

'Now listen,' Anna said, businesslike again. 'I'm trying to get to house number two.'

'*What?*' I was expecting Havana Road. 'Hang on, that's where your parents are.'

'So you found out, huh?' She sighed. 'I have to do this, Stevie.'

A million questions charged into my brain. But this time I didn't try to ask.

'The back of the house is down there.' I pointed over my shoulder.

'I tried that way last night. And ended up in Ray's garden.'

'Ah, what you need is someone to show you, someone local, who happens to be small and quiet,' I suggested.

'That's not what I meant. You've already helped me enough.'

'And I know a boy who'd be a brilliant lookout, very

reliable, well-mannered,' I kept on. 'And afterwards, you can tell me why my name was in the back of your notebook.'

Anna blinked, a slow smile spreading across her face. 'Not so shy and quiet now, are you, Vie?'

It was the first time she'd called me Vie, and I liked it.

*

We managed to get Ray's attention with the very first stone that hit his window. A moment later, he joined us in the yard, coat on over his pyjamas. I caught a waft of supper as the door closed behind him.

'Couldn't sleep anyway,' he whispered.

Inside the house, someone flushed the toilet. We looked up in alarm.

'S'all right, it's just Mum – *again*,' Ray muttered. 'She thinks we'll have to go to the nuclear bunker tomorrow. She's worried sick.'

We crept out into the alley where it was safer to talk. The supper smell was still there, stronger if anything. It wasn't coming from Ray, I realised, but from Anna.

'What *is* that?' I asked, sniffing the air.

'Leftovers,' Anna replied, taking from her coat something wrapped in a Bagatelli's white napkin. Now

I understood why she'd patted her pocket just now. 'For my dog.'

I stared at her. '*Your* dog?'

'Aha!' Ray grinned. '*Now* I get it!'

'He's called Cyril,' Anna told us. 'He's a white boxer, and I need to get him back before I can go.'

'So he's yours? Is he the "thing" you needed to pick up?' Ray looked very pleased: he'd had a hunch about this all along.

'Hang on, we're fetching the dog that attacked Flea?' I was wary, suddenly.

'Sorry about that, Vie, I truly am.' Anna hung her head. 'He escaped from the kennels where my parents left him while they moved house. I was going to sneak him out again—'

'On Wednesday,' I said, thinking out loud. 'From the kennels that's up on Havana Road.'

'Yeah, with a whopping great hole in its fence no one told us about.'

'You weren't at the Co-op, then?' Ray asked.

Anna looked puzzled.

'Oh, never mind.' He seemed pleased that part of his theory had been right, at least. 'Which means that woman we saw last night, with the biscuit tin, was your *mum*?'

'Yeah.'

'Crikey!' Ray muttered. He glanced at me, bewildered. 'And she's caught the dog now, has she?'

Anna nodded. 'After hearing that gunshot last night, I had to check. I couldn't find the way into the right back garden, but I could hear him barking. So what we have to do tonight is sneak Cyril out without waking anyone up.'

It was going to be tricky. I'd lived in one of these houses all my life so I knew how thin the walls were.

Ray was more worried about Cyril. 'He won't bite us, will he?'

'He's never bitten a person, I promise,' Anna replied. 'He probably only went for Flea because he was scared.'

'Of a tiny dog?' Ray wasn't convinced.

'She's a terrier,' I pointed out. 'She probably *did* scare him first, to be fair.'

*

The alley ended in a fork: left took you to the back of Ray's house; go right, follow the path past a few other houses and you'd end up at number two. Here, we left Ray on lookout at the gate.

Like the rest of World's End Close, number two's windows were dark, the curtains closed. Once through the gate, Anna and me dropped on to a patch of lawn as we considered our next move.

'Can't you just walk in? They're your parents, even if you don't want to see them,' I said, unclear why this had to be so difficult. 'And shouldn't they know about the poisoners?'

'You didn't have to help,' Anna answered crisply.

But the fact was, I did.

Anna was our friend. I also knew how much a dog could mean to a person. Even if the world did end when the Russian ships came up against the American blockade, at least Anna would have Cyril with her. And if it didn't, maybe later, after time with her aunt in Wales, she could come home to her parents and work out whatever had gone wrong.

'Where's Cyril likely to be?' I whispered, hoping the soft spot under my right knee was just mud.

'He normally sleeps on my bed.'

'We've got to go indoors?' I swallowed nervously. 'Upstairs?'

'Maybe.'

But Anna's mum and dad would be there. I could almost picture them, two tall, thin people in their dressing gowns, wide awake and worrying about their daughter. Perhaps they were listening for footsteps.

Perhaps the poisoners were after them too.

Now I was scaring myself and had to take a steadying breath.

'We'll check the sheds first,' Anna decided. 'Just in case they've made him sleep outside.'

Getting up off the grass, we tiptoed towards the sheds which stood at right angles to the house. They weren't locked. The first one was full of packing boxes, the second had a very creaky door.

'There'd better not be spiders,' I muttered over Anna's shoulder as she tried to get in.

The door would only open a few inches. Its old hinges made such an awful rasping sound, we quickly abandoned it.

Next we tried the kitchen. The door was on the side of the house, like at ours. But this one was locked.

'Drat it!' Anna cursed.

I crouched down, putting my eye to the lock. The key was gone; I could see right into a room still faintly lit by the coals in the boiler. There was a table, glinting metal chairs, cookery books on a shelf, and weird-looking kitchen gadgets I didn't know the names for.

'Have a look.' I stood up, drew Anna to the door. 'See if you can spot him.'

Anna crouched, her back jammed against my knees

in the small space. I could feel every bone in her spine, every rib. She was shaking too.

'Nope. He's not there.' She sagged against me, then rallied, got to her feet and tugged at her bobble hat. 'We'll have to go in. Can you pick a lock?'

'No. Can you?'

She shook her head, gnawing at her thumb. 'What about the kitchen windows?'

'Too small.'

But there were windows in the sitting room that opened like doors: French windows, was what Mrs Johnson called hers.

Beckoning Anna, I crept round the back of the house again. The French windows were where I expected them to be. The curtains, though, weren't quite long enough to reach the floor. I got down on my knees, pressed my face to the glass. The room was dark, the outline of a settee, a chair, a table just about visible. Suddenly, at eye level, a pink, squishy nose appeared. The shock made me tumble backwards.

'Cyril!' Anna rushed to the window.

The pink nose became a flurry of jowls, ears, chunky white shoulders. She hadn't needed cold meat to bribe him. Cyril, totally overjoyed, scrabbled at the glass with his paws: I was terrified he was going to break it. Anna tried to shush him. The whole door was shaking. Worse still, inside the house, a light snapped on and a woman called out, 'Cyril? What are you up to?'

'We'd better go,' I told Anna.

'I can't leave him, not now he's seen me,' she begged.

But I didn't want to get caught. That had never been in the plan.

'We'll find another way to get him out,' I promised.

As Anna stood up, Cyril jumped, throwing his whole weight against the door. There was a ting as the bolt gave way. The door shuddered, then wobbled open just enough for a huge head to push its way through. Anna grabbed his collar as the woman's voice called again, 'How did you get that door open, you naughty—?'

We didn't hear the rest. We had Cyril, and were running for the gate.

Day Five

THE WORLD HOLDS ITS BREATH

The Daily Times, Saturday 27 October 1962

19

At breakfast, Nan insisted we keep the radio on.

'In case they've found that poor Anna Burgess,' she said.

'You love a drama, don't you, Nan?' Bev remarked.

Yet we both felt guilty about the story we were hiding. Bev hadn't touched her toast, and I could only nibble around the edges of mine. I kept thinking about Anna on her way to Wales – whether she'd caught her train yet, or if Cyril the boxer dog was behaving himself. Or maybe, like Nan had said, the trains weren't running properly, and everything was messed up for Anna and our mum, on her way back from Liverpool.

When, finally, the morning news came on, that was equally bleak. There was no mention of Anna. Everything was about Cuba – last-minute peace talks, or, if they failed, whether the Russians or Americans would fire first. I gave up on my toast entirely at this point.

'Oh lawks,' said Nan, who'd gone pale. 'Let's hope the politicians see sense.'

'*Nan!*' Bev cried. 'There's far more we can do than *that*! It's the anti-war march today, remember? Two o'clock, centre of town, by the war memorial.'

Nan put a hand on her stomach. 'Oh, I don't know, love. People my age don't go on protests. It's not my sort of thing.'

It wasn't exactly *my thing*, either. Me, who barely had the nerve to speak up in class, never mind in a crowd of strangers. But lots of us marching, lots of voices all together, surely that could make a difference? Dr King in America seemed to think so. And hadn't Dad said the best weapon was your voice?

'I'll be there, Bev,' I promised. 'I'll go and check Ray's coming too.'

*

The police car was parked outside number two again. Walking past, I noticed someone had left the front gate off the latch, though it didn't much matter now there was no dog to escape. What did any of it matter, I thought grimly, when we might all be blown up by teatime.

At Ray's house, his brother Pete was standing at the

hallway mirror, combing his quiff to perfection and whistling the new Beatles song. Given the awful news, I was surprised to find him so cheery.

'He's taking his girlfriend to the movies, that's why,' Ray told me, pulling a face.

Pete caught my eye in the reflection and grinned. 'And what about you two skivers? Any more dodgy capers planned for today?'

'What *capers*?' I asked, flustering. How the heck did Pete know we'd missed school? Had Ray told him? Or was it Rachel?

Before anyone could say more, the front gate squeaked open. Sergeant Mukherjee came up the path with a determined look on his face.

'In here, quick!' Ray pulled me into the sitting room. Luckily, we could still hear everything through the closed door.

'Morning, Elvis,' Sergeant Mukherjee said to Pete. 'Can you find your father for me?'

'He's not here, sorry. He's doing overtime. The airbase is on high alert,' Pete replied.

'Ah, right. Your mother, then.'

'Sure, I'll find her,' Pete said brightly. 'But hey, please don't call me Elvis.'

*

Sergeant Mukherjee, Mrs Johnson and Rachel swept into the sitting room so quickly, we'd only just managed to move back from the door. Like at our house last night, the policeman was the one person in the room who didn't sit down. It made me nervous all over again.

'I'll be brief,' Sergeant Mukherjee said, taking off his hat and smoothing his hair. 'I'm here to ask a favour – of you, miss.'

He was looking directly at Rachel. What he wanted was for her to take part in a police reconstruction of Anna Burgess's last known movements, he explained, which they'd be filming this morning in the town centre. Admittedly Rachel was shorter than Anna, and rather *darker*, as Sergeant Mukherjee carefully put it, but she was of a similar slim build. And with the right clothes, in the right place, it might be enough to jog someone's memory.

'Someone must have seen Anna Burgess,' the sergeant insisted. 'Someone knows where she is.'

I tapped my foot. Ray was biting his lip. Rachel leaned forward in her seat, like a diver at the edge of a pool. I willed her not to say anything: just one wrong word and it would all be over.

‘They’ve given us a slot on the evening news tonight – unless anything more . . .’ the sergeant paused, ‘. . . *dramatic* happens over Cuba.’

Mrs Johnson agreed Rachel could take part.

‘Though we must be back by lunchtime,’ she insisted. Her eyes flicked to the far corner of the room where a suitcase lay open. Inside were sweaters, toothbrushes, a clutch of books.

I shuddered, suddenly cold. Mrs Johnson was packing for the airbase bunker, wasn’t she? Ray said they’d be going there today if the Cuba situation worsened.

‘Not a problem, Mrs Johnson,’ Sergeant Mukherjee assured her. ‘We have to be finished by noon, anyway, because the town centre is being closed off for the peace protest this afternoon.’

But what about the poisoners? I wanted to ask. Why hadn’t the police mentioned that Anna was being followed? What were they doing about *that*?

Yet saying anything would prove we knew Anna. We had to keep quiet. I still worried Rachel wouldn’t manage it, and the second we were out of earshot, Ray and I reminded her.

‘You’re not to say a single *thing* about Anna. You don’t know her. You’ve never seen her before, all right?’ I said firmly.

'Just do what the policeman says, and keep quiet,' Ray insisted.

Rachel looked at us both, pityingly. 'Honestly, I'm a very good actress. That's why they've asked me to do this.'

When Mrs Johnson reappeared, she was wearing lipstick and face powder, and her best blue felt hat.

'Coat on, Ray, and you, Rachel. Sergeant Mukherjee's coming by to pick us up.'

'Are we going in the police car?' Rachel's eyes went dinner-plate round. 'Can Stevie come too?'

'I say she should,' Ray agreed.

Mrs Johnson hesitated. 'There might not be room in the car.'

'Don't worry,' I said. Though, of course, I desperately wanted to go with them, to find out what Anna had been up to that day she arrived in our town. And it must've been obvious, because Rachel seized my arm, tucking it firmly through hers.

'You let me come with you yesterday,' she whispered. 'Fair's fair.'

So when Sergeant Mukherjee drew up outside with a toot of his horn, Mrs Johnson took the front seat, and we bundled ourselves into the back.

*

Half an hour later, on the other side of town, we found ourselves standing in front of the hospital building. This, bizarrely, was where Anna's parents had last seen her.

'She must've been visiting a sick relative,' Ray guessed.

'She never mentioned one. And she didn't seem to know the place when we passed it on the bus, yesterday,' I replied, though all it proved was how little Anna had told us about herself. We barely knew our friend, that was the truth of it.

Already, a sizeable crowd was gathering outside the hospital. White-coated doctors, nurses in blue uniforms, members of the public were spilling off the hospital drive and on to the lawns that lay either side. There were hundreds of worried people here, all wanting to find Anna.

And us three, who knew where she'd gone. It was impossible not to feel outnumbered.

Meanwhile, after the initial rush to get here, we waited – and waited – for the filming to start. Mrs Johnson and Sergeant Mukherjee disappeared somewhere to make the final arrangements, so we stayed with Rachel, who was too excited to stand still. She'd seen a man with a huge television camera, and was convinced this was going to be her lucky break for stardom.

'Not everybody has a TV set, so the audience might not be huge,' Ray pointed out gently. 'But it's a great way to start.'

'I just hope Mr Reilly from school is watching,' Rachel answered, tossing her curls. 'He'll be kicking himself he didn't pick me for the play.'

Something in the crowd caught her attention.

'Oooh! See those people?' She pointed, brazenly, at a man and woman walking towards us.

The woman, wearing an apple-green cape and matching hat, was thanking people for coming, shaking hands, kissing cheeks. A couple of steps behind was a man with a huge, rust-coloured beard.

'That's Anna's mum and dad,' Rachel told us. 'Sergeant Mukherjee's been talking to them for ages.'

'Oh heck,' Ray muttered. 'They're coming over!'

'We can't speak to them!' I cried.

My mouth had already gone bone-dry. As for my face, they'd only have to look at me to see the guilt all over it. And what if they'd spotted me in their garden last night? What if they recognised me?

I ducked down, but it was too late: they'd already reached us, Mrs Burgess so close I could smell her perfume. She greeted Rachel with a hug, then shook Ray's hand. She smiled at me briefly, but it was Rachel who had her attention, much to my relief.

'Thank you so much for doing this, Rachel,' Mrs Burgess told her, smiling and teary at the same time. 'I'm sure you'll be terrific.'

Painful though it was, I couldn't help staring. Anna's mother was tall and slim like her daughter, but not a bit like her in her manner. Mrs Burgess was all clipped vowels and matching accessories. It was Mr Burgess who was more like Anna, I decided. He hung back, fidgeting, looking over our heads as if he'd rather be somewhere else. Nan would think the Burgesses were 'pound-noteish', which was her funny way of saying a person was posh. But what surprised me most was how normal they both seemed, like the sort of people you'd pass every day in the street.

So why *had* their daughter run away? I wondered, yet again. And did Mr and Mrs Burgess know how much danger Anna was in?

*

Finally, after the long wait, Mrs Johnson returned with Sergeant Mukherjee. A nice policewoman who took

Rachel off to get changed. Filming was due to start in ten minutes.

Rachel returned wearing maroon trousers, a short black coat and a pea-green woolly hat, with her long hair hidden underneath. Even from a distance, I couldn't see much similarity to Anna. The clothes were wrong too – the wrong shape, the wrong colours.

Mrs Burgess, though, was speechless.

'That's exactly how she looked when I last saw her!' she gasped, immediately in tears.

Mr Burgess muttered something into his beard.

The cameraman then started telling people where to stand. The pavement had to be clear for Rachel to walk along it, so everyone was ordered to shuffle back. Standing near Mr and Mrs Burgess meant we were very near the front. We gave Rachel a 'good luck' thumbs up as she moved into position.

Excitement – or something like it – stirred in me, too. We were about to discover what our mysterious friend had been up to in the hours before she'd arrived at my coal shed.

'Are you ready?' I whispered to Ray.

'Abso-blooming-lutely,' he replied.

The cameraman raised his arm to signal he was ready too. Once Sergeant Mukherjee was in position, he started speaking directly into the television camera. Cap in place, jacket neatly buttoned, he looked reliable, solid, the sort of person you could depend on.

'So far, what we know of Anna Burgess's disappearance is this . . .'

20

At seven o'clock on Tuesday morning of this week, Anna and her parents had caught the train from their old home in Essex. At the station, they'd taken the 6A bus to the hospital, a journey of no more than ten minutes across town. They got off at the stop before the hospital to check into the Cherry Lane Hotel, where they'd booked rooms until Friday, after which they were moving into a house in World's End Close on the eastern side of town. Together, they left for the short walk to the hospital at about 10.45 a.m. Mr Burgess, deciding he'd like a newspaper, sent Anna back to the newsagent's they'd just passed to buy a copy of *The Times*. He didn't have the right change so gave her a five-pound note.

Mr and Mrs Burgess kept walking slowly, expecting their daughter to catch them up. The route took them along the main road, past the Debenhams' offices and the telephone exchange, before turning right towards the hospital. Their appointment was at eleven o'clock.

The doctor, who was a specialist in blood disorders, had been running some new tests.

On Anna.

I glanced at Ray: *Anna?*

He gave a tiny shrug, as baffled as I was.

Yesterday, it'd crossed my mind that Anna looked peaky – she slept a lot on the bus, and had still seemed really tired. But a blood disorder sounded serious. And, I began to realise, scarily familiar. Though no one had put an exact name to it, there'd been something badly wrong with my dad's blood, as well.

The Burgess family knew Anna was worried about the hospital appointment, the sergeant went on. She hadn't slept well the night before. She hadn't eaten breakfast that morning. But her mother said it wasn't unusual for her daughter to be nervous, because she hated hospitals.

When Anna didn't return with her father's newspaper, Mr Burgess went back to the newsagent's himself. No one fitting Anna's description had been in the shop. Maybe she'd gone to the other newsagent's further down the road? But Mr Burgess checked that one too.

Alarm bells were ringing now. They searched the hospital. The bus station, the train station, the hotel. No one had seen their tall, bobble-hatted daughter. And no one, to their knowledge, had seen her since. There was also the small issue of Anna's dog escaping from the boarding kennels where he'd been staying during the house move, and again last night from the family home. The local dog warden had been informed.

There the trail went cold.

'Okay, cut!' The cameraman stopped filming.

Sergeant Mukherjee's shoulders relaxed, and he moved off to talk to Anna's parents.

'When's it my turn?' Rachel wanted to know.

'Five minutes, ducks,' the cameraman called. 'We're having a quick break.'

Ray blew out his cheeks, turning to me. 'What d'you make of all that?'

'I'd never have guessed she was ill,' I admitted, keeping my voice low. 'Not serious, hospital-type ill, anyway.'

'Hmmm. No one's mentioned the arsenic yet, have they?'

'Or why they decided to move to our street, when it's the other side of town from the hospital.'

The five-minute break was over. Now it was Rachel's turn in front of the camera. After a few shots of the family at the bus stop, the cameraman filmed Rachel, walking alone. Now, for the first time, she reminded me of Anna, right down to the way she swung her arms and took big, gangly strides.

'Your sister's acting is pretty good, isn't it?' I told Ray.

At one point, it felt as if I was watching the real Anna walk down the street. And it struck me how sad and lost she looked. Maybe all she'd needed that morning of the hospital visit was someone just to ask her if this was what she wanted, if she was okay.

*

Once filming was over, the hospital staff went back to their wards and clinics, and the crowds began to thin out. All around us, conversation switched from Anna Burgess to the peace march. It was encouraging to hear just how many people were going along.

'It might not make one jot of difference,' a man in a flat cap was saying. 'But if we all join together, then we're harder to ignore.'

'I'm not one for protests, myself,' the woman with him replied. 'But what else can we do?'

'Quite right, love. None of us wants this crazy war, do we?' another woman chipped in.

I turned to Ray. 'You'll come on the march, won't you? I meant to ask you earlier, sorry.'

'S'all right.' He kicked the pavement moodily. 'I can't come, though.'

'Oh.' I'd hoped he would, especially after what he said yesterday about Dr King, and this was a peaceful protest.

'I mean, I *want* to go, especially after reading your dad's letter,' Ray added, sounding thoroughly fed up. 'But I can't imagine Mum letting me.'

Nor could I, to be honest, especially with that suitcase in the sitting room, and her insisting they had to be home by lunchtime. The nuclear bunker plan was obviously a real possibility. The thought of Ray disappearing underground for three months didn't bear thinking about.

'Fancy a gobstopper?' I asked, just to change the subject.

*

By the time we'd returned from the newsagent's, gobstoppers fizzing in our cheeks, Rachel was in her own clothes again.

'Did I do all right?' she said in a low voice.

'You were brilliant,' I said, and slipped into her pocket the pink sugar mouse we'd bought her because Ray said it was her favourite.

All the way to the bus stop, Mrs Johnson kept touching Rachel's shoulder, her hair, or straightening the lapels on her coat, as if she was grateful *her* daughter was still here. It must be nice, I thought, to have a mum so affectionate. But even if mine didn't hug much, it still felt better when she was here. I was so looking forward to her coming home.

Just as we turned the corner for the bus stop, we saw the cameraman packing his equipment into the boot of a waiting car. The car doors were open, the radio humming away inside.

'Excuse me, mister, will we be on the news tonight?' Rachel called out.

The cameraman straightened up, turning around to see who was speaking.

'Not likely now, ducks,' he answered grimly.

The nice policewoman from earlier was sitting in the car's front seat, listening to the radio. Her hands covered her mouth, as if she'd just heard something terrible.

'Why, what's happened?' Mrs Johnson asked, fear in her voice.

'An American pilot's been shot down over Cuba, by the Russians.'

My breakfast slid around in my stomach.

'But the Americans and Russians are making a last-minute deal, aren't they?' Ray asked.

I'd heard the same thing on the morning news.

'Yeah, but they can't agree on it. And now this pilot has been killed, some are saying the first shots of the war have already been fired.'

Mrs Johnson took Rachel's hand.

'Time to go,' she insisted.

We hurried along the street towards the bus stop.

'Let's hope no one pushes the nuclear button,' Ray said through gritted teeth.

'Is there an *actual* button?' Rachel asked.

'How should I know? Honestly!' Mrs Johnson cried. 'Can we please talk about something else for a second!'

But no one could think of anything to say. My head was full. There'd be a red flashing switch, surely, with 'DO NOT TOUCH' on it in bold letters. Or a series of codes to punch in, a special camera that photographed your eye.

Who would do it, though? Kennedy? Khrushchev?

Who'd want to be remembered for ending the world?

No one would remember it, that was the thing. We'd all be dust.

21

With no one in at my house, Ray said I should come to his. In the kitchen, we huddled around the radio to hear the latest news for ourselves. The cameraman was right – an American pilot's plane had been shot down by the enemy. Someone from the government came on air next, saying surely the Americans would retaliate now. Everything was tipping towards war.

'Join us later for the evening news update … if we're still here, that is,' the newsreader signed off.

'Flippant so and so,' Mrs Johnson muttered.

She switched off the radio. Pushing her glasses up her nose, she turned to us, all the colour gone from her face. It made me think of Miss Elliott running from our classroom, and how frightening it was when the grown-ups you trusted got scared themselves. I'd gone beyond being scared, though: I felt numb.

'Ray, Rachel, go upstairs to your bedrooms. Choose one thing to bring with you,' Mrs Johnson said, the fear there again in her voice. 'And make sure it's small. We're only taking one suitcase.'

'Why, Mum, where are we going?' Rachel asked.

It was the hopeful way she said it that made me suddenly want to cry, as if after her exciting morning, she'd forgotten about the bunker.

'I'm sorry, Stevie,' Mrs Johnson said, unable to look at me. 'We can't take you with us. It's airbase workers' families only. You'll have to go home.'

Somehow, I pushed myself up out of the chair. It wasn't that I wanted to go to the bunker: what floored me was I'd now have to say goodbye to Ray.

He was on his feet too.

'I'm walking Vie home,' he announced, and, taking my arm, steered me to the door.

'Five minutes, then we're leaving!' Mrs Johnson called after us.

*

We stopped outside my front gate, like we'd done a million times before. Only this time we were trying not to cry.

'You know this stupid war might not even happen, don't you?' Ray reminded me. 'So make sure you do your maths homework, because it'll be school as normal on Monday, I bet you.'

For once it was a lovely thought.

'And you'll call round for me, eight o'clock on the dot?' I asked.

Ray nodded. 'Same as always. Don't forget to set your alarm clock – sorry, *clocks*.'

I couldn't quite manage a smile.

'I just hope my mum makes it home and Anna gets to Wales,' I said.

'Gosh, yes, your mum *has* to get back. And Anna has to be okay.' Ray rubbed his arm across his eyes. 'Look, we've just got to hope that President Kennedy—'

'Ray,' I stopped him. I didn't want our last conversation to be about presidents or war. 'Remember when we thought our street was the most boring place on the planet?'

'Yup!' He tried to laugh but couldn't.

'Well, look at it now.'

I didn't usually pay much attention to World's End Close, but that moment, as I stood beside Ray, the houses looked bolder, more real, as if someone had outlined them in black pen. There were no dogs barking, no birds singing. The early sun had gone and the sky was overcast, the only faint, background noise someone's radio covering the Saturday football game which was playing on, regardless.

The quiet was shattered by a scooter turning into the street.

'I'd better go,' Ray muttered, but didn't move as the scooter pulled up alongside us.

A young man climbed off and removed his crash helmet. The blond, feathery hair and twinkly blue eyes belonged to Gary the Mod, Bev's old boyfriend.

'She's not in,' I told him.

Gary looked past me, just like he'd always done.

'Well, she's here now,' he remarked, giving his hair an extra fluff.

I turned to see Bev running back into the close. She was coming from the direction of the waste ground.

'There you are!' she cried, rushing towards us.

Gary went confidently to meet her, but she ran straight past him to me and Ray.

'She's still there, up at the pillbox.' Bev tried to catch her breath. 'After what you told me last night, I went to check.'

My jaw dropped.

'But Anna caught a train early this morning.' Ray stared at Bev, at me. '*Didn't she?*'

'Not unless she's got a twin,' Bev replied. 'You'd better

get up there. She's asking for you both, though I'm warning you, she's not in good shape.'

Aware of Gary earwigging, I pulled Bev to one side.

'Is she ill? Has she eaten something bad?' I asked. Despite what we'd found out at the hospital this morning, the poisoners, I was sure of it, were still Anna's biggest danger.

'I don't know what's wrong with her,' Bev answered, sidestepping me. 'Go and see for yourself. Sorry, Vie, I've got to dash. The march is about to start and it's going to be bigger and better than ever.'

She then noticed Gary. 'Are you coming along to wave a banner?'

Gary smirked, shook his head. 'Now listen, babe—'

'Is that a no?' Bev said impatiently. 'Because if it is, then you'd better clear off!'

*

I'd forgotten how dark it was inside the pillbox. Anna was lying on the bed of leaves underneath Ray's sleeping bag and blanket, and the sprawled-out body of a snoring dog. She tried to sit up when she saw us.

'Move yourself, Cyril,' she groaned, which set her off coughing. The dog woke up with a grunt.

‘What happened? Did you miss the train?’ I asked, kneeling down beside her.

Ray kept his distance, his attention half on Cyril, who was now on his feet and coming to say hello.

‘Ah no, I’ve gone and got the stupid flu, haven’t I?’ Anna croaked.

All that sleeping on the bus, and still being tired – she’d been coming down with it yesterday, hadn’t she? Or was it to do with the blood disorder? I didn’t know. But what she needed was a warm, dry bed, not a damp nest of leaves in a pillbox.

‘You should be indoors with that throat,’ Ray said, clearly thinking the same.

Anna smiled weakly. ‘You sound just like my mother.’

I didn’t smile back. Nor did Ray: Mrs Burgess in tears over her missing daughter was still too fresh in our minds.

‘The police made a reconstruction about you this morning,’ Ray tried again. ‘You’re going to be on the news. You’re more famous round here than President Kennedy.’

Anna’s laugh quickly turned into another rattling cough. When she’d finished, she lay back and shut her eyes. She really wasn’t well and it worried me.

'Come to my house,' I decided. 'Bev's on the peace march, Nan's out with Flea, so no one's in. You can sleep in my bed if you like.'

Anna's eyes opened slightly. 'What's the point? There's a war about to start. People are out looking for me. It's over as far as I'm concerned.'

'You can't give up now! You've got Cyril back, that's what you came here for. Once you're well again, you can still go to Wales.'

'And what if the world doesn't end?' Ray pointed out. 'What if no one pushes the button, and life goes on?'

Anna pulled the blanket around her shoulders and turned to the wall.

'Leave me alone,' she mumbled.

That made me angry.

'People care about you, Anna,' I cried. 'Your mum – your dad – us. So stop being so ruddy selfish, and let us help you.'

'I . . . can't . . . I . . . oh . . . it's . . . it's all such a mess!'

Her shoulders began to shake, and when she turned back to us she was crying. She'd come close to it a few times since we'd known her, but I'd never seen her like this, tears streaming off her face and into the pillow.

Ray gave her another of his almost-clean hankies.

Then, as gently as we could, we helped her to sit up, then stand. She didn't have the strength to argue any more, and Cyril came quite happily as we made our way out into the daylight.

*

Not wanting to risk being seen in the street, we squeezed into our garden through the back hedge. I went first, just to double-check no one was in. The house was empty and nicely warm. Cyril, meanwhile, was tied up outside, with a bowl of water, some biscuits and an old blanket. I didn't think Nan would want him indoors, and Flea certainly wouldn't. In the kitchen, Anna gulped down two big glasses of orange squash, but didn't want any food. She'd taken off her black coat, and underneath her clothes looked dirty and crumpled. Her teeth chattered with cold.

'Here.' I handed Ray a hot-water bottle. 'Fill this, will you? The kettle's still warm.'

Upstairs, I found Anna a pair of my pyjamas. They were far too short, of course, the trousers ending halfway up her legs. It was then I noticed the bruises. They weren't the normal kind you'd get from falling off your bike. These were livid-purple, green and yellow splodges all over her calves, and they brought a lump to my throat because Dad had had bruising just like it.

Not wanting to stare – or cry – I got to work on my bed. Without Mum here to remind me, I hadn't made it this morning. But once Ray and me had plumped the pillows and turned down the flannelette sheets, it looked pretty inviting. When Anna collapsed into it, she let out the longest, most delicious sigh.

I pulled up a chair next to the bed.

'Do you want me to stay with you?' I asked. 'Just in case?'

'In case of what?' Anna yawned.

'In case the poisoners come.'

Anna laughed weakly. 'I don't need a bodyguard!'

'What about the peace march?' Ray reminded me. 'You've got to go. You promised Bev.'

And my dad, I thought.

'Well, you've got to go to the bunker,' I answered.

Ray's jaw clenched.

'If you don't mind,' Anna said, pulling the blankets up to her chin, 'I'd like to go to sleep, so kindly take your discussion somewhere else.'

I got up to leave, but Ray didn't move. 'Tell us who the poisoners are, Anna, then we'll go.'

'You probably know them already,' Anna replied sleepily. 'And their real names.'

I caught Ray's eye: *did* we?

We certainly knew more about Anna than we did earlier. She was scared of the hospital, so her parents said. She didn't want any injections or treatment. Perhaps to her the medicine they were trying to give her felt like a poison – like arsenic.

'Your mum and dad are the poisoners, aren't they?' I realised.

'*What?*' Ray's mouth fell open.

I almost expected Anna not to answer. But she gave a nod.

'They'll still try to make me, as soon as they find me,' she said.

'Make you what?' I wanted to know.

But her breathing had changed: she'd fallen asleep. She looked so ill, so thin, lying there on the bed. I couldn't help but think of what Dad said about magic pills and how badly he wanted to recover.

'She's got to get better,' I gulped, fighting back the tears. 'We've got to try and save her.'

Ray nudged me. 'Then we'd better start by saving the world, hadn't we, eh?'

'The peace march, you mean?'

'Exactly. I'm coming with you.'

'You are?' Though it made perfect sense that he was. 'Oh, Ray, that's abso-blooming-lutely brilliant! Come on, or we'll miss the start.'

But Ray, being Ray, had to speak to his mother first.

22

Mrs Johnson flung open the front door before we'd even reached it.

'Where the devil have you been?' she demanded.

I was standing behind Ray, and saw him draw his shoulder blades together.

'I want to go with Stevie, on the march,' he replied.

The silence was like the seconds before a thunderclap. I peered out from behind Ray at Rachel, who was sitting at the bottom of the stairs, the suitcase at her feet. She caught my eye and winced.

'Please shut the front door, Stevie,' Mrs Johnson instructed.

I did as she asked, and though I wasn't sure which side of it she wanted me on, I stuck with Ray.

'We've been waiting nearly an hour for you. Your dad's expecting us up at the airbase,' Mrs Johnson said, struggling not to raise her voice. 'Now say goodbye to Stevie and fetch your coat.'

Ray didn't move.

'I'm warning you, Ray. Don't make this any harder than it already is. Get your coat and hurry up. I won't ask you again.'

Ray, to his credit, didn't back down.

'What's the point in hiding away, when we could be doing something about it?' he answered.

Mrs Johnson pushed her glasses up her nose, which was never a good sign.

'It's a march for peace, Mum, that's all,' Ray tried to tell her.

'What would your father say, eh?' Mrs Johnson was getting angry now. 'He's an American, or had you forgotten that? It's him you should be supporting, not a load of troublemakers in town.'

'I'm not a troublemaker, Mrs Johnson,' I insisted. 'Nor's my sister.'

'See? It's not about communists or capitalists or whose side you're on,' Ray argued, sounding impressively like Bev. 'No one's going to win a war like this.'

Mrs Johnson pressed her lips together. She wasn't about to change her mind. It was pointless.

'Well, if you won't listen to me . . .' Ray shot past his mother, stepped over Rachel and bounded up the stairs.

He came back down with a letter on blue airmail

paper. I guessed – correctly – it was from his cousin Violet in America.

'. . . perhaps you'll listen to Violet,' Ray said.

His eyes snaked down through the letter until he found the bit he wanted to read. 'Here it is: "I know you'll want to go to college one day, cuz, so hear this awesome news – the very first black student has enrolled at the University of Mississippi to study politics . . ."'

He stopped. Looked hopefully at his mum.

Mrs Johnson took her glasses off and rubbed her face with both hands.

'I don't know, Ray, what you're trying to tell me,' she said. 'But it's got nothing to do with today's march.'

'It's got *everything* to do with it,' Ray hit back. 'The university let that student in because of Rosa Parks, the Montgomery Bus Boycott, Dr King. All those people protesting and speaking out against what was wrong in America. They didn't give up, and Dad wouldn't want us to give up, either, not for something so important.'

It seemed to me he was making a very strong case. But Mrs Johnson didn't appear to think so.

'You're not going to change my mind with a letter,' she said.

'A letter changed *my* mind – ask Stevie what her dad said about nuclear bombs! Go on!' Ray answered.

It caught me off guard, rather.

Mrs Johnson simply shook her head. 'I don't think Violet meant for us—'

'MUM!' Ray cried, exasperated. 'There won't be any cousin Violet, or Dad, or you or me or anything, if this war happens.'

I sidestepped out from behind Ray.

'Please, Mrs Johnson,' I tried. 'You could come with us if you wanted. You might enjoy it.'

'I'm coming.' Rachel was already on her feet, reaching for her coat.

Ray gestured for me to open the door. I half expected Mrs Johnson to explode, or block the way to stop us leaving. Instead, she huffed on her glasses, wiped them on her skirt and put them back on. And when she looked at me, I glimpsed the brave young woman who'd stood on the beach at Budmouth Point all those years ago, sticking her neck out for what was right.

'We can't go on a march without banners, can we?' she declared.

Within minutes there was a tablecloth, pillowcases, and every coloured felt-tip pen in existence spread out on the living-room floor.

'Wow! She didn't take much persuading!' Rachel whispered as their mother went to fetch more pillowcases.

'Our mum's still a rebel on the quiet,' Ray replied. 'I bet she wanted to come all along.'

*

The bus dropped us outside Lipton's on the high street; between us, Ray and I manoeuvred our banner down the steps. We'd used Mrs Johnson's old tablecloth so it was a whopper of a sign, even in its rolled-up state. I was heart-burstingly proud of what it said.

At first, town was relatively quiet for a Saturday afternoon, apart from the evening-paper sellers who were yelling across the street to each other as if it was some sort of contest:

'Black Saturday: United States Prepares for All-out War,' shouted one on the street corner.

'Read all about it,' hollered another on the opposite side of the road. 'Spy Plane Shot Down Over Cuba: Major Rudolf Anderson First Casualty of War.'

The headlines were terrifying. Everywhere, the newspapers were already nearly sold out, and a van was pulling up to the kerb to unload more copies.

'Don't look, Vie,' Ray advised, hurrying me past.

I'd already stopped worrying about the 'whats' and 'woulds' and 'maybes' of this silly, pointless war. It was the words of Dad's letter that filled my head now, each one a little flame, a little star of hope. I could feel myself standing a bit taller. And with my free hand I pushed my fringe back determinedly from my eyes.

As we walked, the street grew steadily busier. Like us, most people were heading in the direction of the war memorial, where the march was due to start. Everyone seemed in good spirits. I saw posters, signs, lots of CND badges like Bev's, and it made me want to open our banner and wave it, proudly.

'Now?' I asked Ray.

'Not yet. Save it till we actually get there,' Ray replied. But he was eager too, standing on tiptoe to see how much further it was to the memorial.

Poor Rachel was clinging to her mother's arm and looking uncharacteristically worried, as if the whole Cuban situation had finally hit her.

'It's not too late, is it?' she was asking. 'We can still make a difference?'

'Always,' Mrs Johnson assured her. 'Don't let any politician tell you otherwise.'

Up ahead, where the road narrowed, the crowds grew

even thicker, a blur of faces, banners, hand-painted signs. The noise of drums, voices chanting, singing, shouting, echoed off the buildings and made me wonder just how many people were here. It was like match day at the football ground, only ten times louder. The feeling, the buzz of it, hit us like a wave.

I looked at Ray. 'Now?'

He grinned. 'Now!'

We unrolled the banner, apologising to anyone we bumped. The words, black against the white damask cloth, were Dad's.

THE BEST WEAPON IS YOUR VOICE

Ray held one end of the banner, while I held the other. We'd stiffened the sides with pea sticks from the garden, so it would hang properly, but Ray being taller than me meant it still looked a bit wonky.

'That's terrific!' Mrs Johnson cried, stepping back to admire our handiwork. 'Just up a bit, Stevie, there, that's level.'

Once Rachel and Mrs Johnson had their own signs sorted, we set off again. The crowds closed in around us. The police, lining the pavements, chatted with the protesters. People passed round cakes and bags of sweets as they walked. It felt like being part of a carnival or a celebration. Our banner was a life raft, keeping Ray and me together as we clung to our respective ends. Every few steps, we'd share an excited, bewildered *don't you dare let go* look, though we knew we wouldn't.

'Look, Stevie!' Rachel pointed, suddenly. 'It's your nan!'

'I'd be surprised,' I answered. All I could see were people's shoulders, the backs of heads.

Rachel was insistent. 'It *is* her! There! Just past Boots!'

I still couldn't see who she meant, and was pretty sure she'd made a mistake. Nan wasn't the protesting type: she'd said so herself. And even in crowds like these, anyone in a red paisley scarf and leopard-print coat should be relatively easy to spot. I'd been hoping to find Bev and gave up on that idea too. The street had turned into a river of drum-playing, banner-waving, hand-holding, chanting people. The current carried us along.

'One, two, three, four, we don't want your chuffing war!'

As we turned into North Street, I spotted Meena from school. And just in front of her, Harvey Brooker, putting his big mouth to good use for a change. Tanya was there too, with more of the girls from our class. I didn't hesitate to wave. Tanya smiled and raised her banner at me. Meena waved back with both hands. From then on, I kept seeing people I knew – people I'd never in a million years have expected to be here. Mrs Talbot from the paper shop, Miss Elliott our class teacher, and even Dr Elson, the headmaster, who'd obviously changed his mind about nuclear bombs.

Normally, I didn't speak much to any of these people. Yet here I was – here we all were – using our voices to say the same thing. Being part of something so big, so powerful, and with so many other people, made you feel big and powerful yourself. Safe inside the crowd, I felt I could do anything. Maybe I could even save the world.

Yet the biggest surprise came next when, about ten yards away, I saw the back of a very familiar quiff. It was Ray's brother Pete. No one else I knew wore a leather jacket with a white T-shirt and their hair combed up at the front – unless you counted James Dean and Marlon Brando, but they were faces on the wall at Bagatelli's, and not real people.

Pete was meeting his new girlfriend today, I remembered, seeing a girl standing with him. She had dark, bobbed hair, this girl, and between them her and Pete were waving a huge 'BAN THE BOMB' banner, painted in red letters on a striped bed sheet, just like the ones on mine and Bev's beds at home.

Come to think of it, the girl looked an awful lot like Bev. And when she turned sideways, I realised it was Bev.

I laughed out loud.

'Yuck!' Ray groaned. But he saw the funny side of it too.

Never in a month of Sundays would I have put them together. Bev liked parkas and Lambrettas, The Who, The Beatles: she had posters of them on her wall. What Mods didn't like, *supposedly*, were rockers – and that's what Pete was, with his love of rock 'n' roll and turned-up denim jeans.

Trying our best to keep with Mrs Johnson and Rachel, we shuffled towards the two lovebirds.

'Are you the new girlfriend, then?' I asked, once I was close enough to tap Bev's shoulder.

She spun round, startled. 'Oh, Vie, hello!'

Pete was smiling, a smudge of Bev's frosted-pink lipstick on his cheek. Mrs Johnson reached up to wipe it off, pretending to disapprove.

'Mods and rockers, eh?' She tried not to smile. 'Who'd have thought it? There's hope for world peace yet.'

It was as if the weather agreed, because for the first time that grey, bleak October afternoon, sunshine seeped through the clouds.

23

Eventually, the march brought us to the steps of the town hall, where, so Bev told us, Important Local People were going to give speeches. I half expected my sister to be one of them: she'd protested at school, made banners, spread the word about the march, which made her very important in my mind. Plus she had a new boyfriend, who she'd probably want to impress.

Yet when I asked, she looked horrified.

'Give a speech? Me, in front of all these people? Not likely!'

It hadn't occurred to me that sometimes even Bev would rather keep her opinions to herself. Though, to be fair, it was a massive crowd.

The first person to speak was a man with beige hair, beige trousers and a short beige raincoat. Apparently, he was our local MP. The megaphone he was using made him sound tinny, like he was commentating on a swimming gala. None of us could hear him properly, though you didn't need to – it was obvious from people's reactions how quickly the crowd was losing interest.

Pete, who was the tallest, stood on tiptoe, hand cupped to his ear in an attempt to listen.

'He's telling everyone to go home!' Pete reported back to us. 'He's saying we should trust the government to handle it. Says there's nothing we can do – who the heck *is* this guy?!'

'Your local MP, who people voted for,' Mrs Johnson reminded us, bitterly.

The tinny megaphone voice petered out. From the front of the crowd came a cheer.

'Hang on!' Pete was up on tiptoe again. 'He's giving someone else a go. He's handing over the megaphone!'

Now things were taking a more exciting turn, I stood as tall as I could to try and see what was happening. The crowd was cheering and whistling. I joined in, excited, because whoever it was had to be better than a dull politician.

Yet when the person made her way up the town hall steps, and I caught sight of a leopard-print coat, my entire body went cold. Stuffed in the front of the coat, head poking out like a baby kangaroo, was Flea.

'Oh. My. Word!' Ray gasped. 'That's your *nan*!'

I groaned. 'And my dog!'

'Told you I'd seen her,' Rachel said smugly.

Bev let go of Pete long enough to stare, hands on hips, in amazement.

'What the heck is she *doing* up there?' she cried.

I'd no idea but I dearly wished she'd get down. We watched in horror as Nan took the megaphone, tested it, then gave it back to the MP. She turned to face the enormous crowd.

'Oh no,' Bev muttered. 'She's going to give a speech, isn't she?'

I nodded, wincing.

'I'm not one for marches, but today is important,' she began, in a voice big enough to reach up the street. 'Some wars are necessary – we needed to beat Hitler, didn't we?'

'Bravo for pointing out the bleeding obvious!' a man shouted.

'As I was *saying*,' Nan went on, glaring at the heckler, 'I'm not the protesting type. But sometimes something comes along that isn't about politics or who you vote for. Sometimes you just know something isn't right, though it takes a bit of courage to speak up.

'And soon you realise you're not the only one thinking it . . . and what you're feeling starts to grow. What you're saying gets louder.'

Despite the horrid embarrassment of it all, I noticed that people had stopped fidgeting and calling out. They seemed to be listening.

'There'll be those who won't like what you're saying. My granddaughter got the cane at school yesterday for protesting about the war. But I wasn't cross with her.' Nan shook her head for emphasis. 'No, I'm proud that our young people are speaking out.'

A cheer went up.

Bev rolled her eyes, blushed, just about managed a smile.

'When things are so obviously wrong – and this war, if it happens, will be a flipping disaster – then we have to speak out. Don't be shy, don't worry about what your neighbours think,' Nan went on.

Mrs Johnson straightened her shoulders. Next to me, Ray gave me a nudge.

'She's not bad, your nan,' he whispered.

I nudged him back, thinking the same. I was even beginning to enjoy myself.

Then Nan mentioned Dad.

'My son was in the army for many years. He was a good man, proud of his country. But he knew things about these bombs – terrible things he never talked about, but if he was here now he'd tell you . . .'

I wasn't expecting this: it threw me completely. The

MP, who'd been cringing on the sidelines until now, rushed towards Nan.

'All right, that's quite enough,' he cried. The crowd started jeering again: it was hard to hear or see what was going on.

'You'd better get up there, Bev. Make sure your nan's okay,' Mrs Johnson advised.

Bev tucked her hair nervously behind her ears. 'I'm . . . not sure I can, Mrs Johnson. I'm not good in front of big crowds.'

Nor was I. But I found myself offering to go.

'She's my nan too,' I retorted when Ray tried to stop me.

The crowd was so deep, it was like crawling through a forest of legs and arms.

'Excuse me, please! Excuse me!' I cried, battling my way through.

It took ages to get even halfway to the front. Then a few yards from Nan, suddenly, people were moving out of my way. The crowd surged, pushing me forward, on to the first of the town hall steps.

A few steps above me Nan was locked in an argument with the MP.

'It's a peaceful protest, so why shouldn't I?' she was yelling.

'Please stop pointing your finger at me!' cried the MP.

'Nan!' I beckoned furiously, hoping she'd see me and come away.

She did see me – or at least Flea did, and sprang out of Nan's coat. Nan stumbled back as the crowd laughed, then went 'awww!' I managed to scoop Flea up, feeling her heartbeat against my hands. Or maybe it was mine, because I could feel that too, going like a hammer in my chest.

'Take your grandmother home, there's a good girl,' the MP begged.

Nan squared up to him. 'Now just a minute, you . . . !'

'She's only saying what's true!' I blurted out, and climbed the last few steps between us. 'About the bombs. My dad wrote a letter to me, explaining all about it.'

'Aha!' Now Nan's full attention was on me. 'So he *did* tell someone in the end!'

A strange quiet had fallen over everyone, especially the people right at the front. When I looked down they were staring at us, fixated, waiting for someone to speak.

'What was in the letter, love? Go on,' a woman with her hair in plaits urged.

I could feel myself sweating as I shifted Flea on to my other hip. All I wanted was to get Nan off the steps. But Dad said if anyone ever threatened to use nuclear weapons, I should speak up. Since reading his letter I'd been wondering what to do with all that information – just telling Ray hadn't been enough. Maybe *this* was what I had to do, up here on the town hall steps. If I sloped off now, with so many people listening, I'd be letting Dad down, I knew it.

'My dad . . .' I began.

'Speak up, love!' a man yelled.

'Can't hear you back here!' someone else shouted.

My face was burning, my mouth felt clumsy. Nan grabbed the megaphone from the MP and passed it to me, but I didn't think it would help. I hated talking to an audience: I hated speaking up in class. I couldn't think like that now, though. I tried not to look at the strangers' faces staring back at me, at the crowd that spread right up the street. Instead, I looked for Ray and our banner. And when I found him – though the tablecloth hung limp, and I could only see the word 'voice' – it was enough to give me a grain of courage.

I tried again, louder this time.

'My dad saw nuclear bombs being tested. He . . . he was told never to tell anyone what he'd seen and to forget about it, but he couldn't. It stuck in his head until he—'

I pushed my fringe back, and began to look up, properly.

'– well, he called them peaceful bombs before he saw one tested, because he was told they'd never be used: they were just meant to scare people. Then he saw one go off, and he had to clean up afterwards – all the dead birds, and the black rain that fell out of the sky.

'When he came home … he got ill. The doctors thought he'd been poisoned, but didn't know what by. He wrote a letter I found in an old suitcase, about …' My voice began to crack. 'th … three weeks before he died.'

Nan slipped her arm around my shoulders. Suddenly it felt as if she was holding me up.

'He said …' I gulped, 'a person's voice was their best weapon. I …'

I buried my face in Flea's fur. I couldn't say any more. The quiet held on for a few gentle moments, then, at the front, people began to clap. The sound spread as fast as fire through the crowd. When I dared to look up again, everyone as far as the eye could see was applauding.

'There you are,' Nan said proudly.

'It's not for me,' I told her. 'It's for Dad.'

'It's for being brave, that's what.'

I laughed, though I was crying, too. 'Well, I'm never doing it again, that's for sure!'

24

Soon after that, the protest ended and the streets began emptying. Posters and banners were stuffed into overflowing waste bins, people squeezed in and spilled out of the nearest pubs, and I stood on the pavement, still stunned at what I'd just done.

'Gee whizz, Vie, you were ace!' Ray gushed. 'You got up there, and you showed 'em!'

'Wasn't she a diamond? Did justice to her poor dad's memory, she did,' Nan said.

'She was WOW.' Rachel beamed. 'Just WOW.'

I squirmed, happily embarrassed.

Bev then did something that we didn't do enough of in our family: she gave me the biggest, warmest hug.

'Listen, shortie, you were brilliant,' she whispered.

Then everyone's attention switched to the Radio Rentals shopfront across the street. In the huge bay window, thirty television screens flashed up the latest news. Thirty President Kennedys stared back at us, then thirty Russian warships, streaming across the Atlantic Ocean towards Cuba and the American blockade of boats. Arrows on a map showed how far apart they were – hours at most. And when those warships met the blockade, what would happen if both sides still refused to back down?

Mrs Johnson gave my arm a squeeze.

'You've done your bit, Stevie,' she assured me.

That didn't stop the dread coursing through me all over again.

'It's up to Kennedy and Khrushchev to sort out the rest,' Nan agreed. 'Best we go home and put the kettle on.'

Bev and Pete decided they'd still rather go on their date to the Plaza for the early evening film. The rest of us made our way to the nearest bus stop, heads down, hands in pockets, anxious and quiet. Ray and me hung back a bit from the others. We needed to decide what to do about Anna. It was almost a relief to have something else to focus on.

'What are we going to do if she's too ill to move?' Ray asked. 'I mean, your mum's due back today.'

'And she won't be impressed to find a stranger in her bed,' I agreed.

Ray looked worried. '*Should* we tell the police now? Is it time?'

I hesitated. There were still a few policemen and women about on the streets. We could walk up to one, right away, and tell them everything. It was probably the grown-up, sensible thing to do now everything had got so complicated. We couldn't hide Anna forever. Yet just because it was complicated and difficult, didn't mean we had to give up.

'Remember what Anna said about being in charge of her destiny?' I said.

Ray nodded.

'I think Anna should be the one deciding what happens next.'

And so, on the short bus ride home, we came up with a Plan A and a wobbly Plan B to suggest to her. Plan A was simpler: it involved aspirins, hot soup and extra blankets, and sneaking Anna out of the house by whichever route was clear. We'd make the pillbox shelter more comfortable, somehow, until she was strong enough to leave to go to Wales. If the Russians or Americans dropped their terrible bombs, then obviously the plan wouldn't work. Nor would Plan B, or any plan, come to that.

*

Back at my house, we found Anna pretty much as we'd left her, still asleep in bed.

'Let's move her now, while there's no one in,' Ray suggested, because Nan was still out in the street, gassing with Mrs Johnson.

'Good idea.'

At the sound of our voices, Anna's eyes fluttered open.

'This is getting to be a habit, you two catching me asleep,' Anna remarked. Pulling the covers around her shoulders, she turned over as if she was going back to sleep.

'Anna,' I pressed. 'Are you feeling better? Well enough to go back to the pillbox?'

'Huh?' She lifted her head off the pillow.

'We need to move you. But don't worry, we've got—'

'Shhhh!' Ray pointed frantically at the floor.

Noises from downstairs – a kitchen cupboard creaking open, heels clacking across the kitchen lino – told us Nan was back indoors.

Ray caught my eye: Plan B it was.

Plan B was trickier, mainly because we'd not yet worked it out. What I was supposed to do was go downstairs and distract Nan, while Ray slipped out through the front door with Anna. But I suddenly remembered we'd left Cyril in the back yard. Also,

Anna's parents' house was in full view of our front door: we hadn't factored either into the plan.

Anna, meanwhile, had drifted off to sleep again. I gave the bed a shake.

'Please, Anna, you need to get up,' I begged.

Anna opened her eyes and propped herself up on her elbows. The effort made her cough. It wasn't a quiet cough, either, but a proper *hack hack hack* that I worried Nan would hear downstairs.

I grabbed Anna's clothes, which were in an untidy heap on the floor, then told Ray to wait around the other side of the wardrobe.

'Can you get dressed?' I asked her.

''Course I can,' she croaked.

But it took all her strength to pull the jumper over her head, and when it came to the trousers and shoes, I had to help. Finally, breathing heavily, she was ready. But I was beginning to get a bad feeling about this, and when I called Ray back again, he took one look at Anna and shook his head.

'We've got to try,' I urged him.

Anna stood up slowly. She put on the coat I held out for her. Then the bobble hat. Chin up, shoulders back, she took a shaky breath.

'Are you sure you want to do this?' Ray asked her, very

gently. 'Because you don't have to, you know. Remember, you get to choose.'

She looked at him, stunned, like he'd just offered her the moon.

Tears sprang into her eyes, spilling down her face, on to her coat. She swayed a little. Righted herself against the chair. Then, almost gracefully, her great, long legs buckled under her, and we caught her just in time before she hit the floor with a thump.

Between us, we managed to get Anna back on to the bed. She looked so white, so frail, I felt properly afraid. How could we save her, really? It was a stupid idea to even try.

Yet despite the tears still dripping off her chin, Anna was smiling.

'Can you give me a minute?' she said.

Downstairs, another door creaked. Voices murmured on the radio. I caught Ray's eye: did we *have* a minute? Ray shrugged helplessly: we didn't have much choice.

'Listen to me, both of you,' Anna said slowly, clearly. 'I've decided to stop running away. I'm tired of it. I've had enough.'

Ray blew out a huge breath. I felt myself sagging, and reached for the edge of the bed.

'You're proper ill, aren't you? This isn't just the flu,' I said.

'You could say that, yeah.'

'The police said it's a blood disorder.'

'That's it. My stupid, dumb, good-for-nothing blood. The doctors have run out of ideas for making me better.'

I tried not to think about what this meant.

'What are you going to do?' Ray asked her.

'That's the bit I'm still trying to work out. Back in Essex I didn't have that many friends, not ones I could really count on, you know? But since I've met you two, it's been different. I've had to count on you and you haven't let me down, not once.'

My face warmed. Ray smiled his funny, upside-down smile.

'So what I've got to do . . .' Anna took a deep breath, then rolled her shoulders like a fighter, 'is get my act together and try to trust the other people in my life who want to help me.'

'Like the doctors, you mean, at the hospital?' I asked.

She nodded. 'And my mum and dad.'

'What about the arsenic?' Ray wanted to know. 'Was that *really* true?'

'Sure it was,' Anna replied. 'It's used in all sorts of medical treatment, so they—'

A scream from downstairs cut her off.

The scream was quickly followed by a yell, a laugh.

And Nan calling up the stairs, 'Where are you, Vie? Come and hear this, quick!'

Ray froze. 'Geez! What do we do now?'

I groaned, head in hands. This was all happening too fast.

'Vie?' Nan called again, then as if she was talking to someone else, 'She *is* up there, somewhere.'

There were footsteps on the stairs. More laughter. Someone hurrying along the landing, first to my bedroom at the back, then stopping to shout:

'Vie?'

My heart jumped in my chest. 'It's my mum!'

'I think we've blown any escape plans, haven't we?' Anna decided, burrowing back under the covers.

A swish as the bedroom door opened.

'What the heck's that wardrobe doing there?' I heard Mum say.

She appeared from behind it, still wearing her best coat. I leaped up off the bed, so glad to see her.

'It's a bit of a long story,' I confessed, knowing I was about to be in awful trouble.

But Mum was laughing – and crying – as she took my hand and kissed it. In her other hand, she was holding the little radio that normally sat on the kitchen windowsill.

‘The Russian boats have turned back, love!’ she said, waving the radio in the air. ‘They’ve just announced it on the news!’

I didn’t quite believing what she was saying. ‘So is it over? There’s not going to be a war?’

‘No war. No more missiles. The Russians and Americans have made up.’

I burst out laughing, which quickly turned into tears. It must’ve been the relief of it all, and having Mum here, holding my hand. She didn’t mind when I leaned against her. She smelled of laundry soap and our kitchen. And when she wrapped her arms around me, for the first time in ages, I felt truly, totally safe.

‘They’ve made peace? There’s not going to be a war? I can’t believe it!’ Ray was clutching his head, looking dazed.

Letting go of Mum, I gave Ray a hug too. Just a quick, awkward one, until it got embarrassing. We sprang apart, then giggled, nudged each other, all the usual stuff.

Mum, meanwhile, had moved around to the head of the bed. She was still smiling, but in a different, rather puzzled way.

‘Since the world’s not about to end, you’d better tell me who *you* are, dear,’ she said. ‘And why on earth you’re in my bed.’

Anna sat up. She took off the bobble hat, her hair fine and tufty underneath. When she gazed up at Mum, her eyes were huge, burning, fierce.

'I'm Anna Burgess and my parents have reported me missing,' she answered. 'I think I need to see a doctor, please, and then I'd like to go home.'

*

Much, much later Mum relented enough to let me go to Ray's before bedtime. Pete was still out courting our Bev, but the rest of the Johnsons were in the kitchen. It was about time, I decided, to stop feeling shy when I came here, and to smile when they all turned my way to say hello.

Mr Johnson was at the stove, making big, fat American pancakes.

'Hey there, Stevie!' He waved. 'Come on in, grab a seat!'

I did, gladly, and not only because of the pancakes. A tugging sensation in my chest told me I needed to be with Ray, and Rachel, and Mrs Johnson. It was the comfort of knowing they understood what we'd been through these last few days, that I wouldn't have to explain myself, because they'd be trying to get their heads round it too.

The Cuban situation was still the hot topic.

'What did the Russians and Americans agree on in the end?' Ray wanted to know.

'The Russian missiles won't stay in Cuba, and the Americans are taking theirs out of Turkey,' Mrs Johnson told him.

'I didn't know there *were* missiles in Turkey.' Ray looked worried.

'Best not to think about it too much,' his mum reasoned. 'There's been give and take on both sides. There's no winner, not in this situation.'

'Some arguments aren't about winning, son,' Mr Johnson added. 'Sometimes it's all about knowing the right time to stop fighting and start talking.'

After pancakes, Rachel insisted on singing 'The Star-spangled Banner' to us at full volume. Mrs Johnson, fingers in ears, was trying to follow the evening news on the television.

'No point in watching it, our police reconstruction won't be on,' Rachel stopped singing long enough to say. She sounded disappointed.

'They don't need to show it now Anna's gone home,' I pointed out. 'Which is a *very good thing*.'

And it truly was. I'd been there, with Anna, when her parents had arrived. Her mum had been in such a hurry to reach her daughter, she'd walloped her shoulder on the corner of the wardrobe. Anna's dad fell to his knees beside the bed. There'd been tears, angry words, and Anna dissolving into a fit of coughing. Mum hurried me downstairs at that point. The doctor was due, and as we waited for him, Mum finally got cross with me.

'What on earth did you and Ray think you were playing at?' she demanded. Not pausing for me to answer, she went on about how Anna's poor mum and dad must've been sick with worry, and how sometimes I didn't have the sense I was born with.

'I go away for a few days, and this happens. Was *anyone* in charge here?' Mum asked.

'Don't blame me,' Nan said defensively. 'I didn't have a clue there was a girl living in your coal shed, at least not until the fruit cake went missing.'

I stared at my hands.

Mum softened enough to tell me she knew I'd meant well in helping Anna, and that I'd done it in good heart.

'Just like her dad, isn't she?' Nan remarked.

Mum sighed sadly, pushing the fringe off my face. 'She is.' And, for the second time that afternoon, she hugged me.

It was our usual family doctor, Dr Gibley, who came, wearing his trademark spotty bow tie and crumpled trousers. If he realised just how ill Anna was, he didn't show it. He stayed calm and composed, took out a stethoscope, a thermometer and those things that looked like lollipop sticks, then confirmed a chest infection. He left Anna with a bottle of bright pink medicine.

Through all of this, Mr Burgess said very little. He perched at the bottom of the bed, rubbing Anna's feet so gently it brought a lump to my throat. After the doctor had gone, Cyril was finally allowed upstairs. At first, he wouldn't stop wriggling and snorting. But as Anna's medicine began to work, he finally settled enough to spend the next few hours lying beside her like a stone dog on a nobleman's tomb.

Later, when Anna woke up, she was well enough to go home. Already, she seemed different – not healthy, exactly, but the hard, determined set of her face had been replaced by something calmer, more hopeful.

'D'you think she'll be okay – with her parents, I mean?' Ray asked, after I'd told him all this.

'Yup, I do,' I answered. 'If the Americans and Russians can sort things out, it makes you realise that even the most horrible arguments can be fixed. The hard bit is being brave enough to start talking.'

DAY SIX

PEACE DEAL STRUCK AT
ELEVENTH HOUR

The Weekend Times, Sunday 28
October 1962

25

'I've been wondering,' Mum said, the next morning. 'What if Mr and Mrs Burgess and Anna had somewhere neutral to talk their problems through?'

We were at the kitchen table, drinking tea, and Mum had just been telling us about her conflict resolution course. I still wasn't sure I understood it totally, but I liked the idea of people listening to each other.

Bev narrowed her eyes, thinking. 'D'you mean the Burgesses could meet here?'

'And Mum could be the referee?' I guessed.

'That's not *quite* how it works, love,' Mum answered. 'It's more about talking through a disagreement – and hearing the other person's point of view.'

But Bev knew what I meant, and winked at me.

'Whatever it is,' I agreed, 'it's got to be worth a try.'

*

I wasn't sure the Burgess family would accept the invitation, but they did, surprisingly readily, and a time of two o'clock was agreed.

'I can help – make the tea, pass the biscuits and so on,' Nan offered.

'But there won't be enough chairs if we're all here,' Mum replied.

It wasn't strictly true, but was probably Mum's way of keeping the meeting small and quiet. So Bev, quite happily, went off to call for Pete. And Nan declared, somewhat sniffily, that it was time she went home, anyway, because her houseplants would be gasping. I helped her carry her enormous suitcase as far as the bus stop.

'You know, I'm glad I missed my darts night and came to stay,' Nan said as we hugged goodbye. 'Though it's been a right old week, hasn't it, eh?'

'Promise you'll come over soon?' I asked.

She gave me a twinkly smile. 'Just for a cup of tea, mind. I couldn't cope with all that drama again – or another week sleeping in your bed.'

Back at home, without Nan, the house felt different – emptier, almost. It was quieter too, and not just because the radio had stayed off. The Burgess family meeting was to take place in the sitting room we rarely used. Though

Nan hadn't understood why we didn't go in there much, I was, at last, beginning to. When the door opened it made a kissing sound like a seal being broken on a tomb.

'Burgess, Burgess,' Mum muttered as we gave the room a quick dust. On the wall were my parents' wedding pictures, and there was a cabinet for Bev's school prizes and the silver cup Dad won at the local flower show for his King Edward potatoes. 'I'm sure I know that name from somewhere.'

'Anna knew us too,' I told her. 'She had our name and address written down in a notebook.'

'Really? That's interesting.' Mum paused for a second, duster in hand.

I agreed it was.

*

At two o'clock sharp, the Burgess family arrived. Anna looked much brighter after a good night's sleep and a few doses of Dr Gibley's pink medicine. Soon enough, she was sitting on our settee, saying yes please to a cup of tea and could she have two sugars in it. She wore a blue pinafore dress and a striped woolly hat I'd not seen before. I felt a bit shy at first, being here together, indoors, with everyone else. But when the grown-ups weren't looking, she gave me a daft Scout salute, so I knew she was still the same Anna, still my friend. Cyril lay at Anna's feet, doing his best impression of a noble tomb hound. We thought it best to keep Flea in the kitchen.

'We're very grateful to you,' Mrs Burgess said to Mum. 'And so very relieved to have our girl home.'

Anna's parents were sitting either side of their daughter. Her mum, smart and glamorous, was rather like President Kennedy's famous wife. Her dad, quieter, rarely looked up from his hands.

Without Bev or Nan, the job of serving tea fell to me. I found some Bourbon biscuits in the larder and came back with the tea tray just as things were getting started.

'You went with your parents to the hospital on Tuesday morning?' Mum was asking Anna. 'And the next day you were moving house? That must've been stressful.'

It had been a fair old week for all of us, Nan was right. Once everyone had their cups of tea, I was glad just to sit out of the way and listen.

Anna inspected her fingernails. It was Mrs Burgess who answered Mum.

'First Anna disappeared, then our dog escaped from the kennels. We didn't get the house keys until Wednesday in the end. There was a mix-up over the paperwork – all our post went to the wrong address. So yes,' Mrs Burgess answered with a tight smile, 'you could say it was rather stressful.'

'Anna still shouldn't have run off like that. There's no excuse for what she's put us through.' Mr Burgess spoke in a quiet voice, but stirred his tea so angrily it slopped into the saucer.

'Perhaps we should hear your daughter's version?' Mum asked, and because Anna still hadn't replied to the question, she put it to her again. 'Anna, how did you feel on Tuesday morning? Something must've really upset you to make you run away.'

Anna raised her chin. It was a look I knew all too well, especially where questions were concerned.

'What's there to say? I hate hospitals,' Anna replied. 'That's it. I hate blood tests, I hate needles, I hate people in white coats talking about me over the top of my head.'

'Anna, darling,' her mother soothed, reaching for her hand. 'They're doing all they can.'

Anna pulled away.

'Well, I wish they wouldn't bother,' she replied sharply. 'What's the point? You know they can't cure it. You've heard them say so, and I heard it too, so stop pretending.'

It was a shock to hear her say it, properly, out loud.

Yet, all along, it'd been obvious – in how thin she was, the bruises, the lack of hair and eyebrows, the fact she was often tired. I'd known what it meant, even when I'd hoped it was just a dose of flu and that helping Anna run away would solve everything. I'd recognised the signs, of course I had, because I'd seen it before with Dad. But it still didn't prepare me for feeling as if I'd been walloped in the chest.

Mum kept Anna talking: 'Tell us what happened on Tuesday morning.'

I glanced at Mr Burgess, who was tapping his fingers on the arm of the settee.

'Dad wanted a newspaper,' Anna explained. 'He's been following the Cuban missile story – obsessing about it—'

'*Obsessing?*' Mr Burgess interrupted. 'You do realise what damage those weapons can do?'

I did, and took a hasty sip of tea to stop my mouth going dry. Mum probably knew too – she'd been the one who'd kept Dad's letter all this time.

'It was a terribly serious situation,' Mum reasoned. 'Hardly surprising your father would want to keep up with what was happening.'

Anna shrugged irritably. 'Why? It's just more bad news. And that's what the hospital would've told us too: bad news. I've had enough of it.'

There was a beat of silence. Mrs Burgess twisted her hands nervously. Mr Burgess stared straight ahead at the chimney breast. When he spoke again, he sounded calmer, clearer.

'The doctors want to give the treatment another go, Anna. Yes, it's highly toxic and not without risks, but it's our only hope,' he said.

'But I'm not getting any better, am I?' Anna argued.

'We can't wait for a miracle.'

'No, you're not listening to me.' She was firm. 'You and Mum, you want me to keep trying, to keep taking stuff that doesn't work. But what about what *I* want?'

'We're scared, darling, that's all,' her mum said quietly.

'So am I, Mum!' Anna cried. 'Just the thought of those chemo drugs makes me sick to the pit of my stomach. And now they're talking about trying me on arsenic!'

'The poisoners,' I murmured.

The side effects of chemotherapy were horrible. An image floated into my head of Dad, his thick, curly hair coming out in handfuls. It got everywhere, that hair – on cushions, in the sink. You'd even find clumps of it in your dinner. He hated the treatments, almost as much as being ill in the first place.

Mum got up to open the window. 'What would be

good,' she said, taking her seat again and smoothing her skirt over her knees, 'would be accepting each other's view on this, Mr and Mrs Burgess and Anna, and thinking about how you might move on.'

'How do we do that?' Anna wanted to know, and looked at me, as if pleading for my help.

'Has anyone asked Anna what she actually wants?' I said, because it seemed obvious to me.

Mum shot me a warning glare that I'd overstepped the mark. So it surprised me when Mr Burgess, who was struggling to tear his eyes away from the chimney breast, said, 'She's right, you know.'

He stood up and took a couple of short strides to the fireplace.

'This man knows how hard it all is,' he said, and tapped the glass on one of the pictures that hung above the mantelpiece.

The picture was a photograph of Mum and Dad on their wedding day – Mum wasp-waisted in a long white dress, Dad looking nervous in a suit that was too big for him.

I was rather baffled. Yet something must've clicked in Mum's brain, because her whole face changed. She stared at Mr Burgess, half gasping, half smiling.

'Matthew Burgess!' she cried. 'Of course, it's you.

I thought I recognised your name!'

I glanced at Mr Burgess. At Anna.

'Wait, you know each other?' I asked Mum.

Mum dipped her head. 'We do.'

'We kept in touch, your father and I, when we got back to England,' Mr Burgess explained. 'It helped, having someone else who'd been there, who'd seen those things.'

'You were on the island, watching all those test bombs?'

'Yes.'

'But you didn't get sick?' I pressed him.

'Yes, I did.' For the first time he looked at me properly. His left eye was pale and cloudy. 'Blinded in one eye. Deaf in one ear. But I'm still here, unlike your poor dad.'

'Come and sit down, dear,' Mrs Burgess said gently.

As he took his place on the settee again, Anna shuffled up to make room for him.

'My daughter loves the sea,' Mr Burgess told me.

I nodded: it was one of the things I *did* know about her.

'I wanted to bring her back a souvenir from the island. I always did that, when I went away. But there weren't any shops there, so I brought her home some shells from the beach. Pretty things, they were. And she loved them. She kept them on the shelf above her bed.'

'But the beach was polluted,' I said, remembering Dad's description of the dead fish and black mud.

'I know that now.' Mr Burgess's voice shook. 'No one wants to say so publicly, but I don't believe it's a coincidence that Anna got sick with such a rare illness.'

'We moved here to be near the new hospital,' Mrs Burgess explained, taking over from her husband. 'Your father wasn't treated there, I know, but we told the specialists about him, and they're very interested to see if there is some connection between his illness and Anna's.'

It was a lot to take in for Mum and me. But it certainly cleared up the mystery of why Anna had our surname and address written in the back of her notebook: we were the reason, all along, for her coming to World's End Close. Her parents wanted to speak to Mum – to be close to a team of doctors who knew about Dad.

I suddenly remembered that moment on Budmouth beach, when she'd questioned Ray about his mother, having never once asked me anything about Dad. She didn't need to, I realised now: she already knew his story.

'I'll never forgive myself for bringing home those stupid seashells,' Mr Burgess said.

'A stick of rock would've been better, Dad,' Anna joked bleakly.

Mr Burgess, trying to smile, started crying.

Anna took his hand. 'It's not your fault. No one warned you there'd be fallout from the bombs.'

'No one warned my dad, either,' I said bitterly. 'But if there had been the right treatments around he'd have tried them – he said that too. He wrote it all in a letter to me.'

'Don't suppose you'd let me read it, Vie?' Anna asked.

I glanced at Mum, who smiled as if to say, *It's up to you.*

'Let *your* dad be the one to tell you,' I decided. 'You're lucky, he can explain it all in person.'

But before Mr Burgess could, Flea started barking. Someone was in our kitchen, by the sound of it. I was on my feet to go and check, when the door opened gingerly and Ray's head appeared around it.

'Hello, Ray.' Mum beckoned him inside. 'You know Mr and Mrs Burgess, I expect?'

'It's them I'm here for, actually.' He smiled, a bit sheepish, and handed a blue airmail envelope to Mrs Burgess. 'This got mixed up with our post.'

For a second I thought he was giving her one of Violet's letters, because this one had the same American stamps on it. On this day of strange coincidences, anything felt possible.

Mrs Burgess hesitated before opening it.

'It's from the clinic,' she said, and whispered something up to the ceiling: it might've been a prayer.

On opening the envelope, she shook out the paper. Anna's knuckles were white as she kept hold of her father's hand. Mrs Burgess read the letter twice, before passing it to Anna and Mr Burgess.

'Is it *good* news?' Mum asked tentatively, because we were all holding our breath.

Anna swallowed. 'I think so. It's from a clinic in America. We've been invited over there to try out a brand-new treatment. It's two drugs this time, not just the one, and there's a girl they're treating who's five years old and doing really well.'

I took in what she was saying: at least, I tried my best. Though this treatment was too late for Dad, it might well be just in time for Anna, and that was something good, something to hold on to.

'Where is it in America? Just out of interest,' Ray asked.

Anna looked at the letter again. 'It says the clinic's called St Jude's, in Memphis.'

'Memphis?' Ray's eyes went very wide. 'Wow! The home of the blues! Elvis Presley lives there, though don't tell my brother I know that.'

Typical Ray.

And I had to hand it to him: the timing was perfect, because Anna and her parents, wiped their tears and laughed.

A Few Weeks Later …

26

The world didn't end that week, or the next one, or the next. Normal life returned again: we went to school, watched the gogglebox at Ray's, got excited about a new flavour of crisps called cheese and onion. In fact, you'd almost be forgiven for thinking the Cuban stand-off had never happened.

Yet directly afterwards, just for a day or so, everyone seemed nicer, happier: I suppose it was relief. At the paper shop on Monday morning, Mr Talbot didn't mention that I'd missed last Friday's round. In the corridors at school, the teachers stayed chatting long after the bell for first lessons.

'It *was* close, though, wasn't it?' I overheard Dr Elson say to Mr Jones, the science teacher.

'Doesn't bear thinking about,' he agreed.

I was glad to see Miss Elliott back. She greeted us at the classroom door, wearing a cheerful dress and a smile to match.

'Imagine if it had turned out differently,' Ray whispered as we went in and hung up our coats. 'Imagine waking up today and none of this existed any more.'

'If it meant missing spellings . . .' I replied, because we always had a test first thing on Mondays.

I was joking, of course.

Seeing President Kennedy's picture all over the papers that morning still gave me the collywobbles. It was easier to stick with *not* reading the headlines, at least until the news moved on.

*

Then there was Anna. Despite her now living across the road like a normal neighbour, we barely saw her at first: she was busy getting well for the journey to America, which was planned for a few weeks' time. In a weird way, I missed having her in our coal shed, and often caught myself eyeing up leftovers from our tea, wondering how I could sneak a plateful outside.

Ray said he was glad life had settled down a bit.

'Finally, I can stop thinking every stranger in the street is a poisoner,' he said, with a sigh.

Sometimes I wondered if he was ever truly comfortable with the secret we'd had to keep. But the fact that he'd done it – and done it well – made me proud of my best friend. We'd both had moments where helping Anna had felt too difficult, like we were in a situation that went way over our heads.

Yet who'd have thought he'd stand up to his parents? Persuade his mum to go on a peace rally? And who on earth would've put me up there on those town hall steps, talking to that big, BIG crowd about my dad?

Not me. Never in a trillion years.

The other day, I remembered one of Dad's little sayings: 'When the tide rises, all the boats rise with it', which means if one person gets better at something, it helps everybody. And that was what knowing Anna had done. Her strength had made us discover that we were strong too.

*

Once Anna was feeling better, we were allowed to visit. It was funny going into number two for the first time. On the outside, it was just like our houses. But on the inside, it was all mod cons, as Nan would say. The Burgesses had a television, a washing machine, a telephone, and a machine in the kitchen that made fizzy drinks.

'I think they might be rich,' Ray said under his breath as we sat in a pair of white leather armchairs that made rude noises if you wriggled your bum.

Yet the more we got to know Anna, the more normal to us she became. She was a girl who loved jelly and ice cream, was addicted to quiz shows, knew all the words to Bill Haley's records, and cried if a dog died in a story.

She also had a serious illness, which definitely wasn't normal. And like with Anna herself, we eventually found out its proper name: leukaemia. No one knew for sure if the seashells had caused it, or whether my dad had had the same disease. But the doctors were interested enough to be investigating. Meanwhile, though he was a serious man, with a very serious beard, Mr Burgess was always nice to me, and said how I reminded him of Dad.

On a good day, when the weather was fine, Anna would come out with us for a dog walk. Each walk started with Flea snarling at Cyril, as he tried to sniff her rear end, and Anna so swaddled in coats, jumpers, scarves, she could hardly bend her arms and legs. She'd do stupid zombie impressions, which made us laugh. By the end of the walk, the dogs were fine, and Anna exhausted. For that reason alone, we wouldn't go far – just to the waste ground and back. Every day there'd be more new houses, popping up faster than field mushrooms. Many of the houses already had their roofs on, and Mum said it wouldn't be long before the first one went up for sale.

*

When we weren't visiting Anna or round at Ray's watching *Z-Cars*, he'd come to mine to do homework. We had tests coming up, so Miss Elliott had told us. They were nothing we couldn't handle, nothing we'd not already covered in class. But still Ray and me were dreading them because those tests would decide whether we went to the grammar school in September.

Often, we'd end up sharing the kitchen table with Bev. One night, papers spread in front of her, she sat for ages, just twiddling her pen.

In the end, I asked her, 'Are you stuck on your homework?'

'No, this is my university application,' Bev said proudly.

'What about Pete? You're not leaving him, are you?'

'Stevie . . .' Bev put her pen down. 'Having a boyfriend does not mean I have to give up my brain. I'm going to university, on my own. Nothing's changed.'

Not that Ray was my boyfriend or anything, but I really couldn't imagine starting a new school without him. It'd be like losing an arm, or worse than that – Flea.

It bothered me so much, that I'd started to make an extra-special effort at school, especially with my English. I even asked Nan to get me a book to read from the library.

'A children's book, Nan,' I warned her. 'Not one of those slushy romances you read.'

'Sukie Pengilly happens to be a very good author,' Nan replied crisply.

For once, it was an author I'd actually heard of. And I knew where she lived – in a lighthouse, in a windy place called Budmouth Point. But Nan would want to know *how* I knew, so I kept it to myself.

A few days later Nan came round with a story called *A Little Princess*, and for the first time ever, I read an entire book.

'Can you get me another one?' I begged, when she visited a few days later.

The next book was called *Tarka the Otter*, which really made me cry.

'It was one of your father's favourites as a boy,' Nan informed me.

She'd often say things like this, little snippets about Dad that kept him alive in my head. And Mum was starting to do the same. Better still, Nan was coming over every week now. We'd have tea together, and afterwards sit in the parlour and play Monopoly.

One night our homework was to write a story. It was Ray's favourite type of task, and my absolute worst. Heads down, we both started writing, though it wasn't long before I was stuck, huffing crossly and scribbling things out. Weirdly, though, when I glanced at Ray's work, I'd already written more than him. He kept stopping. And when he'd start again, his pen moved so slowly it was more doodling than writing.

I guessed what he was up to.

'If you're slowing down for me, then don't,' I told him.

'Don't you want us to go to the same school?' he asked, looking confused and hurt.

''Course I do. Just don't hold yourself back for me, that's all. Think about what you want for a change.'

Ray looked at me like I was mad, but as we got on with our work again, I could tell he was thinking over what I'd said.

The next day at school, he put his hand up in class for once. Though Harvey Brooker and Tanya Hardy didn't like how many answers he knew, Miss Elliott was thrilled, so much so she wrote a letter to his parents. And Ray began to realise he didn't have to hide his cleverness, that it was good to speak up, even if it did make some people a bit uncomfortable. His voice had every right to be heard.

*

On a wet Sunday afternoon in November, we said our farewells to Anna. She was leaving for Memphis the next day and invited Ray and me over for goodbye cake. The cake in question was huge, covered in glossy chocolate, and was from the posh bakery in town; Mrs Burgess gave us forks to eat it with. I was on my third slice when Anna said she had a favour to ask.

'Another one?' Ray couldn't help saying.

'I'm asking Stevie, not you. Your track record with dogs isn't exactly brilliant,' Anna reminded him.

Ray grinned. 'Fair point.'

I knew what the favour was, because she'd been gazing mournfully at Cyril all afternoon. And I really felt for her, knowing how much she'd missed her dog the last time they'd been apart.

'Of course I'll look after Cyril,' I told her, before she could ask. 'Flea won't mind. It'll be doggy world peace by the time you get back, just you see.'

Anna leaped up to hug me.

'You are a ruddy godsend, Stevie,' she whispered into my ear.

'Likewise,' I whispered back.

*

After tea had been drunk and cake eaten, Anna needed to rest. Their flight to America was early the next day.

'Can I ask a favour of *you*, Anna?' Ray asked as we zipped up our coats. 'Will you write to us? Stevie and me, we're pretty fond of letters.'

'You know our address,' I added.

World's End Close: it really was a stupid name for a road.

Anna laughed. 'How could I forget it?'

A Few Months Later …

27

It was Monday 4 March 1963 and Mum was right about the snow. By the time we'd left World's End Close for the airport it was already coming down thick and fast. It wasn't a surprise as such; it had hardly stopped snowing since Boxing Day. Still, it was a relief to find the main roads clear enough to not prove tricky for Pete's pride and joy, his new Ford Anglia. Sooner than any of us expected, we reached the sign that said 'Heathrow Airport'.

The flight was leaving at four o'clock that afternoon. It took seven hours to fly across the Atlantic to America. Seven long hours of sitting in a seat, staring out of a tiny window, an overnight stay in a hotel at the airport in New York, then another three-hour flight down south. I was a bit nervous, to be honest, but I didn't tell Ray, because he'd been waiting all his life for this moment. Tomorrow we'd be in America, hearing American accents, paying for things in dollars. That we were going at all still felt like a dream.

Originally, it had been just Ray's father making the trip. His sister Kathryn, who'd lost her husband years ago, was finally getting married again. It was to be a massive church wedding – white dress, flowers, gospel choir, the works – and more than anything, she wanted her brother to walk her down the aisle.

All Ray had done was mention it to Anna in a letter: his dad was going to Huntsville, Alabama, for a family wedding, and though Ray would've have loved to go too, there was no way his parents could afford it. The next thing, Mrs Burgess was on the telephone from Memphis. She was offering to buy plane tickets for Ray and me.

'You'll be flying into Memphis for Huntsville, won't you?' she'd said. 'And you'd be doing Anna such a huge favour. She's coping well with her new treatment, but I can't tell you what a boost it'd be for her to see some friends from home.'

Mum was so stunned by the generous offer, at first she said we couldn't accept.

'But you should see inside the Burgesses' house,' I pleaded. 'They've got white leather chairs and *everything*. Ray reckons they're very rich.'

'Who'll look after the dogs when you're gone?' Mum replied.

'They'll be good,' I said, which we both knew was a

lie. Though Cyril and Flea were great pals these days, sleeping in the same basket, sharing the same dinner dish, they'd learned each other's bad habits, and together could be quite a handful.

It was Bev who managed to twist Mum's arm.

'Are you mad?! It's such an opportunity! You know how much Dad loved travelling – if he was here now, he'd definitely want her to go.'

At which Mum relented, gave me a hug, and said, if Mrs Johnson was happy about it, then she was too.

When we told Mrs Burgess we were coming she begged us not to tell Anna, insisting we should keep it a surprise.

That worried me a little.

'What if Anna doesn't want us there?' I said to Ray, who laughed.

'Stop overthinking. It'll be fine.'

Meanwhile, at Ray's house, Rachel was very upset at the news.

'Why can't *I* go? Violet's the only person who knows how to do my hair properly!' she wailed. 'And Anna's my friend too, you know!'

Quite by luck, the problem was solved when a local theatre company approached her for the main part in their annual play. The girl they'd cast for it had suddenly pulled out, and they wondered if Rachel, who the theatre director had seen being filmed outside the hospital last October, would consider the role? Rachel was thrilled.

The discussions then moved on to how safe Huntsville would be, especially for Mr Johnson and Ray, because things were a whole lot different in America's south. We'd have to be extra careful. Though times were slowly changing, there were still laws that meant Ray and Mr Johnson couldn't sit in the same part of a restaurant as me, or ride with me on a bus. I was horrified when Ray explained it.

'Not as horrified as I am,' he replied.

*

At Heathrow, Pete dropped us directly outside the airport building. The place was a whirl of cars, taxis, people wheeling trolleys, carrying suitcases, women in smart air hostess uniforms. I shivered with excitement. A whole new, busy, *international* world was waiting, just outside the car. And beyond that, aeroplanes, and beyond them, America, Ray's cousin Violet and Anna.

Inside, the terminal was huge and echoey, light from the snowy sky pouring in through the glass roof. There were rows and rows of check-in desks, all with their different airline names and logos – TWA, BOAC, American, Delta – with their staff in colour-co-ordinated uniforms. Since Mr Johnson was looking after the tickets and passports, all I had to do was carry my suitcase. Mum had lent me her best brown one, which almost matched the shoulder bag I'd borrowed from Bev. I'd also had my fringe properly cut and wore the new shoes Nan had bought me for the trip, so was feeling quite smart, for once. Mr Johnson had on his wedding suit, so Ray told me. And Ray himself was wearing a slightly-too-big jacket and tie that had once belonged to Pete.

One look at the other travellers, and it became clear why we'd had to look smart. There was a dress code for travelling by aeroplane. Posh suits, fur stoles, pearls, fashionable hats and perfect lipstick – it was all here, as if people were going to a dinner party or the theatre, rather than sitting in a tin box for seven hours.

It was, I realised, about money. Mum had explained to me these tickets cost hundreds of pounds. Ordinary people like us wouldn't normally be able to afford such a trip. Mr Johnson had saved up hard for his fare: all those extra shifts during the Cuban crisis, bizarrely, probably helped him afford it. Yet there was no way, without Mrs Burgess's generous offer, that Ray and me would have been here now. I couldn't wait to tell her, in person, just how grateful we were.

*

In next to no time we were on the plane. Our seats were near the front, where you could see right into the cockpit, over the shoulder of the pilot to the dashboard full of lit-up switches and dials.

'I hope he's as good a driver as Pete,' I said, with a worried laugh. 'Don't want him mixing the pedals up!'

Mr Johnson leaned forward to ask if I was okay.

'Bit nervous,' I admitted. 'Does it show?'

'Maybe you're just talking a lot more these days,' Mr Johnson replied. 'And it's nice, you know? You got plenty of good things going on in that head of yours.'

When Mr Johnson found out about his wife and kids going on the peace march, he'd not minded as much as we thought. In fact, he started following the civil rights movement in America with a very keen eye. In making plans for this trip there'd been uncertainty about who'd be meeting us at Memphis Municipal Airport. Some of the southern states' airports were still segregated for black and white people, which was when I heard Mr Johnson criticise President Kennedy for being too slow in making the changes he'd promised African Americans.

'The man needs to wake up. Stop dreaming about the space race and the Russians, and start thinking of his own back yard,' Mr Johnson said.

*

Once the plane was full, the front and rear doors were closed. The captain came on the tannoy, his voice an efficient drone of information about wind speeds and altitudes, which Ray clearly found fascinating but baffled me. The hostesses, super sleek, super polite, checked our seats and tables were in the take-off position. The smokers, who'd already filled the cabin with a blue haze, were asked to put out their cigarettes. A great heave and clunk of the brakes, and the plane began to move.

'Is this it?' I asked, bracing myself. 'Is this take-off?'

'Not yet. We're just taxiing out to the runway,' Ray reassured me.

It went on like that for another five minutes – the plane crawling along, stopping then starting again, and me gripping the armrests.

Then the plane turned 180 degrees. The engines changed pitch. They grew louder. And louder. The sound soon became so deafening we covered our ears. The hostesses were signalling to each other to take their seats.

This time, when the plane moved, it shot forward. My head was thrown back against the seat. My stomach felt as if it was still inside the airport building. It was the oddest, weirdest, most thrilling sensation. On either side of me, Ray and Mr Johnson were sitting in the same, slightly stunned way.

The plane picked up speed. The engines screamed. We were hurtling down the runway now, the plane bouncing and shaking like the jets we'd watched at the American airbase that night.

Yet when I squeezed my eyes tightly shut, it wasn't red tail lights I saw, but another airport building, this one in Memphis. There was a sign on the wall saying 'Arrivals', and in among the busy crowds of people hugging and crying and laughing were a tall, skinny white girl – minus her bobble hat – and a darker girl, pretty, with long, braided hair. They'd be standing together, the Burgesses and Ray's Aunt Kathryn, making friends.

When I dared open my eyes, the plane was climbing steeply. We'd already passed through the heavy clouds over London. Now, all that lay between us and America was the biggest, clearest, most dazzling blue sky.

Q & A WITH EMMA CARROLL

What does a day in the life of Emma Carroll look like when you're writing?

I've recently discovered I write better later in the day, which isn't just an excuse for a lie-in, honest! A writing day for me consists of getting up, walking my dogs, doing a couple of hours writing at my desk, then lunch, then writing downstairs on the sofa, surrounded by dogs. I tend to find the first 30k of an early draft the hardest part. My favourite part of the process is editing, because this is when the story thickens up and I can weave in the layers.

What advice would you give to any budding young authors?

Read, read, read. All writers are passionate readers. It's where a lot of inspiration comes from, and where we learn how to craft a story. Also, getting it right takes time. Be patient and let your story grow.

As a former teacher yourself, what advice would you give to teachers about how to develop reading for pleasure – especially historical fiction – in their schools?

Make sure your school has a skilled librarian and a proper library. Model reading to your pupils: the best reading practice I've seen is where the teachers are massively enthusiastic about kids' books, both old and new. Approach historical fiction story-first. This is how I do it as a writer. The adventure, the characters, always come first. The history part of things is world-building, just as it would be in a fantasy novel.

With thanks to Scott Evans (*The Reader Teacher* & #PrimarySchoolBookClub) for writing these questions.

For more resources, head to:
faberchildrens.co.uk

Tell us what you think!
@FaberChildrens